W9-ATW-267

Thale's Folly

By Dorothy Gilman

PUBLISHED BY FAWCETT BOOKS

CARAVAN

UNCERTAIN VOYAGE

A NUN IN THE CLOSET

THE CLAIRVOYANT COUNTESS

THE TIGHTROPE WALKER

INCIDENT AT BADAMYÂ

The Mrs. Pollifax Series

THE UNEXPECTED MRS. POLLIFAX

THE AMAZING MRS. POLLIFAX

THE ELUSIVE MRS. POLLIFAX

A PALM FOR MRS. POLLIFAX

MRS. POLLIFAX ON SAFARI

MRS. POLLIFAX ON THE CHINA STATION

MRS. POLLIFAX AND THE HONG KONG BUDDHA

MRS. POLLIFAX AND THE GOLDEN TRIANGLE

MRS. POLLIFAX AND THE WHIRLING DERVISH

MRS. POLLIFAX AND THE SECOND THIEF

MRS. POLLIFAX PURSUED

MRS. POLLIFAX AND THE LION KILLER

MRS. POLLIFAX, INNOCENT TOURIST

For Young Adults

GIRL IN BUCKSKIN

THE MAZE IN THE HEART OF THE CASTLE

THE BELLS OF FREEDOM

Nonfiction

A NEW KIND OF COUNTRY

Thale's Folly

Dorothy Gilman

BALLANTINE BOOKS

NEW YORK

A Ballantine Book
Published by The Ballantine Publishing Group

Copyright © 1999 by Dorothy Gilman Butters

http://www.randomhouse.com/BB/

Library of Congress Cataloging-in-Publication Data
Gilman, Dorothy, 1923–
Thale's Folly / Dorothy Gilman.
p.   cm.
ISBN 0-449-00364-7 (alk. paper)
I. Title.
PS3557.I433T43   1999
813'.54—dc21   98-27657
CIP

Text design by Ann Gold

Manufactured in the United States of America

First Edition: April 1999

10 9 8 7 6 5 4 3 2 1

1

If a man be anointed with the juice of the herb Rue, the poison of wolf's bane, mushrooms, or todestooles, the biting of serpents, stinging of scorpions, spiders, bees, hornets and wasps will not hurt him. —John Gerard, *The Herball,* 1597

Andrew was bored. He was also—as usual—depressed. About the uncertainties of his future. About this idiotic reentry into his father's world, and certainly about this party he'd been forced to attend. It was the usual corporate affair, but with a number of faux bohemians thrown in, obviously out of a misguided effort to prove how broad-minded the company could be because the party was being held in honor of an author. Xavier Saabo's book was entitled *The Zen of Machinery*— the word *Zen* was big these days—and he was here because in his book he'd said very nice things about Meredith Machines, Inc., and Andrew's father was a vice president of Meredith Machines, Inc.

Which was why Andrew was present—under duress, as usual.

At the moment, with some irony, Andrew was noticing how carefully Xavier ignored the cluster of SoHo guests who

had been invited expressly for him. What no one had fore-
seen, of course—Andrew understood this perfectly—was that
the less affluent contingent were looking upon Xavier with
contempt because he had joined the philistines, and Xavier
was regarding them with contempt because he had long
since exchanged his low-rent loft for an apartment on Park
Avenue.

These musings on the creative life—of which Andrew had
once been a member—were diverted when he saw that Jennifer Tallant had arrived, looking positively seductive in a
black silk sheath. In his several years of college, they had seen
rather a lot of each other until he realized that Jennifer assumed his ambition was to become a corporate VP like his father. He was glad now to see that she was escorted to the
party by Charlie Drumm, who would very definitely become
a VP, if not president of his own company, given time, and
Andrew was thinking kind and charitable thoughts about her
when his father suddenly appeared: tall, fit, silver-haired, and
important. Authoritative, too.

"Andrew," he said sternly, "you're not mingling."

"You mean merging, don't you?" quipped Andrew, since
Meredith Machines was in the process of an important merger with PGH Plastics, Inc.

His father was not amused. "*Mingle*," he said, and turned
away to continue his own mingling.

He and his father had already quarreled earlier in the day.
Summoning Andrew from his cubicle in the nether regions of
the company, where he wrote copy for the *Meredith News-*

letter, also under duress, his father had announced that today was Friday.

"I've noticed," Andrew said warily.

"I've an assignment for you, Andrew," he told him. "Family business."

"Family?" This had puzzled Andrew, for there had not been much family since his mother had left his father seven years ago. There had never been an explanation for this; once upon a time Andrew had assumed that she must have been unfaithful, but now that he knew his father better he thought she need only have found him as much of a machine as those that Meredith produced. What made this difficult for Andrew to understand was that he'd been told that in his youth his father had been a guitar-playing political activist, leading protest marches and working for civil rights, yet somewhere along the way he'd traded those values for profit margins, sales figures, acquisitions, competition, and bottom lines. It was possible at times to feel sorry for him, but not today.

He said again, *"Family?"*

"Yes, I want you to look into property left me by my aunt Harriet Thale. It's in western Massachusetts, about a four-hour drive from Manhattan, and you should be able to wrap it up in a day."

Andrew struggled to remember who this relative could be whom he'd certainly never met. "An aunt Harriet Thale?" he repeated, frowning. "But she died all of five years ago, didn't she? Why this sudden interest *now* in the property?"

"Because," his father said patiently, "I've been paying taxes on one very empty old house surrounded by twenty-five acres, and I've been too busy with the merger to look into it. It's time a decision is made."

"You can't expect me—"

"—to make a decision?" His tone implied that he found his son incapable of any business decision at all. "Of course not. From you I ask for an assessment of what's there. A description. The property's in a godforsaken area, distant from any tourist attractions, but it's time to establish its value so I can decide whether to sell, hold, or whether those twenty-five acres could be developed. Take a camera. It's miles from nowhere but it's time to learn precisely what the situation is."

"Miles from nowhere," Andrew repeated, and suddenly grinned. "I remember now, it was called Thale's Folly! She was the recluse of the family, wasn't she? The family eccentric?"

"She was an embarrassment to us all," snapped his father. "I suppose you think that's amusing."

"I think it's very amusing," Andrew said. "I wish I'd met her. The house is empty?"

"Of course it's empty," growled his father. "You can borrow a company car and leave early tomorrow morning—"

"Tomorrow! You mean *Saturday?*" His father knew very well how precious his two days of freedom were to him.

"—and on your way out my secretary will give you a survey map of Tottsville, the deed describing its boundaries, and directions to Thale's Folly."

Andrew could not help but feel this ridiculous assignment was being presented to him as a subtle form of punishment. His father had patiently seen him through those first days following what he referred to as "Andrew's unfortunate incident"—which did not quite do justice to Andrew's waking up nights in a cold sweat, or the absence of concentration that kept him from what he loved best and had assumed would be his life's work—but he failed to understand why Andrew couldn't simply get *on* with things now.

In a word, he was taking too long to recover.

Which of course was a perfectly rational viewpoint.

As he returned to his dull work of writing copy for the company newsletter Andrew found himself devoutly wishing for a—well, what?

For a less rational world, he thought.

He was to get one.

2

The pith of the [Elder] branches when cut in round, flat shapes, is dipped in oil, lighted and then put to float in a glass of water; its light on Christmas Eve is thought to reveal all the witches and sorcerers in the neighborhood.
—Richard Folkard, *Plant-Lore, Legends and Lyrics*, 1884

Andrew awoke the next morning with the bitter residue of sleeping pills lingering on his palate. Opening his eyes he immediately realized that after five days of mindless work he was being deprived of his free Saturday, and he was convinced that he faced an ill-starred weekend. The horoscope in his morning newspaper agreed with him: *this is a day to remain at home,* it read, *avoiding the small disappointments and aggravations the stars suggest . . . Beware of negative attitudes that will inevitably attract negative events with the force of a magnet.*

Since Andrew could find no way to curb his negative attitude he left defiantly late in the company Mercedes for Massachusetts. He was not surprised, stopping for coffee in Connecticut, when the waitress inadvertently spilled coffee over his jeans.

"Perfectly understandable," he assured her. "My horoscope told me to stay home today."

As he passed the sign welcoming him to the state of Massachusetts, it began to rain, and he discovered the windshield wipers of the car didn't work. While he waited in a garage for them to be repaired and operative again, he pondered his attitude, his father, astrology, and life in general, and noticed that once he was ready to set out again, the rain had perversely stopped and the sun was shining. After lunching in a restaurant just off the Thruway he discovered that he'd left his raincoat behind, and it was necessary to retrace his route five miles to regain it. Once there, leaving the engine of his car running, he dashed into the restaurant, snatched his raincoat from the clothes hook in the hall, and was on his way again, except that as he drove away he saw in his rearview mirror that his action had been misunderstood: a man had rushed out of the restaurant to wave at him hysterically, and then to scribble something—no doubt his license number—on a piece of paper.

Damn cheeky of him, he thought, *they know very well that I paid my bill.*

It was with relief that he finally reached the village of Tottsville, which struck him as too small and unpopulated to inflict any new aggravations. Scarcely a blip on the map, it was extremely rural and looked as if it had long since gone to seed. He passed a few summer cottages along the road with the names of Sunset Roost, Bide-A-Wee, and Rest-A-Wile. Then he passed a ramshackle motel—open, a garage and gas station—closed, and a post office—closed, but with a sign reporting that it was open from 7 A.M. to 12 noon, after which mail deliveries were made. The map he'd been given was on the seat beside him. According to the small penciled X on the survey map, the road to Thale's Folly lay one mile beyond the post office, and on the left side.

Precisely one mile from the post office he spotted a narrow break among the trees and peered into what appeared to be a road, unpaved and uninviting, devoid of any signs of house or human being, and deprived of sun by the trees. An act of faith, he supposed, and with a sigh turned off the highway and entered.

He had not driven far when he saw that his progress was going to be a matter of zigs and zags: four winters of snow and of spring rains had pockmarked and eroded the surface of the road until, "like a blasted minefield," he muttered as he navigated around one serious-looking pothole only to swerve sharply to avoid another. The overgrown arch of trees darkened the road, masking the hollows and making him angry until ahead of him he saw a clear sunlit expanse and stepped on the accelerator; the car shot ahead and then came to an abrupt and shuddering halt.

"*Damn!*" he said in a loud voice, and after finding that neither reverse nor high gear moved the car, he climbed out to assess the situation. Again he said, "Damn!" because the car was leaning to starboard, its right back wheel firmly entrenched—one might almost say half-buried—in a particularly deep and sinister hole. This was surely more than his horoscope had led him to expect. He remembered the garage that he'd passed—closed; he remembered the ramshackle motel, where no doubt there would be a telephone, and somewhere ahead on this road lay the old house and the acreage he was here to inspect.

He had choice.

With a glance at his wristwatch he was surprised to find that it was already after two o'clock, in fact nearly three o'clock. Common sense advised him to walk the two or three miles back to the motel, call for a tow truck, and invest the remaining hours of the day in rescuing the car. On the other hand he would only have to return in the morning to where he was now . . .

He chose Thale's Folly.

Opening the trunk of the car, he dug into his knapsack for notebook and pocket camera, and after locking the car—a purely reflex action, since he felt that if anyone could remove the Mercedes they could damn well have it—he set out down the road to find his great-aunt Harriet Thale's house.

Once divorced from the car, he was surprised to find the air so fresh and filled with all the interesting fragrances of a July day: heat rose from the sun-warmed earth under his feet, and there was a distinct scent of pine. From the jungle of wild sumac lining the road there came the keening cry of a locust; a bird fluttered away, stirring the leaves of an oak tree, and this was followed by a profound silence interrupted only by the patter of the stones dislodged by his shoes; he'd forgotten what silence was like, and he was amused at the thought of its having a sound.

He had nearly passed the house before he noticed the mailbox next to the road, almost suffocated by tall grass and bearing the name of Thale in faded letters. He stopped to look at it, and then he saw the house, set back at a distance from the road among tall trees, its clapboards bleached by the sun into a scabrous silver-gray, its windows nearly blinded by wisteria. Beyond the mailbox lay a driveway, no more than a cart track now, and as he walked up the drive a sudden freshness assailed his nostrils: water, he realized. His father hadn't mentioned a river, pond, or brook, but it would certainly add value to the property. On such a hot afternoon he would appreciate the sound of running water; he might even take off his shoes and wade in it, adding an agreeable dimension to the green woods, blue sky, derelict house, and the astonishing silence, still so utter that he started when he saw a woman seated on the long side porch of the house overlooking the empty field.

It had not occurred to him that anyone would be occupying Thale's Folly, and his father had very definitely said it was empty since his aunt's death. But the woman sat as if she belonged here, propped up in the sun like an attenuated beanpole on which someone had placed a basket of flowers belonging to a hat composed of yards of tulle, at least a dozen chiffon roses, and a cloud of veiling.

A voice from beneath the inverted basket said to him pleasantly, "Good afternoon."

"Good afternoon," he said politely, and waited.

Without moving, the woman shouted, "Gussie? *Gussie!*"

From the bowels of the house came a muffled reply. The woman leaned forward to say confidingly, "She'll come now . . . I am Miss L'Hommedieu."

Puzzled, he said, "How do you do? My name is . . ." He hesitated. His name was Andrew Oliver Thale, but this was obviously a situation that required delicate handling. "My name is Andrew Oliver," he said.

A pair of beady eyes studied him with interest. "You've come about the advertisement?"

The screen door burst open and a woman's voice cried, "What is it now, Miss L'Hommedieu? Leo and I were down in the cellar—" Her voice broke off as she saw Andrew standing in the dust, and her eyes narrowed. She said fiercely, "You're all wrong, we advertised for a younger man. I'm not saying your character's bad but you're too old by at least five years."

A *Gussie, a Miss L'Hommedieu, and an advertisement . . .* "Too old for what?" he asked with interest.

Miss L'Hommedieu chuckled. "I don't think he knows what you're talking about, Gussie."

"I don't, I really don't," Andrew admitted, smiling up at Gussie. She looked fierce, capable, and shrewd, and she wore an apron; definitely his great-aunt's house was inhabited. "My car," he said. "It broke down back on the road."

"Car?" Gussie looked astonished. "Nobody drives this road except the mailman."

"It looked interesting," he said, and with an irony he wished he could share he added, "I hope I'm not trespassing."

"Invite him to dinner," said Miss L'Hommedieu, tugging at Gussie's skirt. "We've got potatoes, haven't we? We'll have fish when Tarragon gets back." The flowered hat quivered as she bent toward the road. "Here she comes now. Ask her."

Andrew turned. A girl was trudging around the rear of the

house carrying a rod and bucket and wearing a pair of shorts and a man's voluminous shirt. He was not prepared for anyone so youthful, and this girl could be no more than eighteen or nineteen. She looked frail under her burden of fishing gear, and he had the most absurd desire to leap forward to carry the bucket for her, but she had already passed him to deposit it on the steps.

"Five," she said, and wiped her face with a corner of her shirttail. It was a small, oval face with delicately modeled cheekbones, a wide tender mouth, and eyes of a startling shade of blue. Her hair had been bleached by the sun into a pale gold, and her skin had been darkened by the sun into a flawless beige just a shade darker than her hair. He realized with astonishment that she was beautiful, and wondered what on earth she was doing here.

"Mr. Oliver, this is Tarragon. Tarragon, say hello to Mr. Oliver."

"Hello," the girl said, ducking her head and starting to enter the house.

Miss L'Hommedieu called after her, "He didn't come about the advertisement, Tarragon."

The girl turned at the door to give Andrew a quick, sidelong, startled glance, and then she was gone, leaving him to wonder just what the advertisement might be that offered her so much relief at not being answered.

Gussie said sternly, "If you're thinking we have a telephone for calling about your car, we don't."

He was not at all surprised by this. "It's all right," he said.

She nodded. "You'd better stay for dinner," and to Miss

L'Hommedieu, "I'll tell Leo he's staying—dinner in forty minutes." Then she, too, vanished into the dim interior of the house.

Andrew glanced at his watch: they would dine at half-past four in the afternoon? He thought of Manhattan, the rituals and the happy hours and the late dinners, but he was distinctly curious now and he reminded himself that a good detective adjusts. Turning to Miss L'Hommedieu he said pleasantly, "You advertised for someone?"

She nodded, beaming. "For a young man, a very *nice* young man, to do light farmwork."

"I see." He felt it extremely thoughtful of them to want to improve his father's property but he wondered if it might not be more thoughtful to let his father know they were here. "You're—uh—planning to develop the farm?"

Miss L'Hommedieu looked shocked. "Good heavens, what gave you that idea? It's for Tarragon, of course."

"For Tarragon?"

She said reprovingly, "We are quite isolated, Mr. Oliver, and it cannot have occurred to you, of course, but Tarragon— you've seen her—has very few opportunities living here. Things are, shall we say, somewhat irregular for her? We are considerably older, as you may have noticed."

He admitted that he had noticed this, yes.

"There is also the—shall I say, uncertainty?—of our future here."

He grinned. "That I can understand, too."

"The problem, then," she continued, "is to find a husband for Tarragon just as soon as we possibly can."

He said in a stunned voice, "A *what*? Good heavens!"

She nodded serenely. "I don't recall who said it—probably Benjamin Franklin, since he said nearly everything—but necessity is the mother of invention. It was Leo's idea. A very clever one, don't you think?"

He said incredulously, "You mean you're advertising in the papers for a young man to work on the farm, but actually you're hoping to marry him off to Tarragon?"

"Oh yes, we are prepared to be quite ruthless for Tarragon's sake."

He shook his head. "It won't work, you know."

"If it doesn't," she told him calmly, "we will let him go at the end of a week—our finances are *extremely* limited—and trust that another will turn up."

"Like a vaccination," he said, fascinated. "If the first doesn't take—"

"A most indelicate way of phrasing it," she told him, "but I am not unaccustomed to vulgarity. You seem a pleasant young man, Mr. Oliver."

"Thank you," he said meekly, "and you may call me Andrew."

"And you may call me Miss L'Hommedieu," she said with a bow of her head that came very near to ejecting several flowers from her hat.

Gussie, arriving at the door, said, "Dinner's served."

Andrew held out his arm to Miss L'Hommedieu and slowly, gravely, she rose from her chair, at which point he discovered that she was almost as tall as his own six feet. He escorted her through the screen door into the kitchen, saying, "I really should wash my hands before dinner."

"There's a basin," she said, pointing to the kitchen sink, and continued on her way without him.

He approached the sink, which had a strange mechanism at its edge that looked surprisingly like a pump of some sort. There was an enamelware basin in the sink; he tipped the water out of it and turned on the faucet. Nothing happened; no water flowed; he realized too late the purpose of the basin he'd emptied, and wiped his hands instead on his jeans. A very odd kitchen, he thought, looking around him and identifying a large woodstove, a small three-burner kerosene camp stove, a huge, well-scrubbed wooden table, and a row of oil lamps on a shelf. Quaint, he decided, and with a shrug he abandoned washing and walked down a hall that smelled of mildew, and into the room on his left.

It was the dining room, and it was dim. Light from its two windows had been all but obliterated by the wisteria outside, and then further diminished by tattered lace curtains that hung like spiderwebs across the glass. In the twilight it was difficult to distinguish the shapes on the table until Gussie brought in a candle and lighted it. Its glow illuminated a white china tureen with steam rising from it in clouds that sent long shadows leaping across the walls.

Gussie said graciously, "I don't believe you've met Leo yet."

Leo, seated at the table, raised his head just long enough to observe Andrew. "Democrat, Republican, or Libertarian?" he snapped.

"Independent," said Andrew.

Leo lost interest and ducked his head again so that only his baldness and the bridge of his nose could be seen. He looked peevish, inquisitive, and very shy.

"You do have electricity," Andrew suggested, his glance returning to the candle as he seated himself.

"Oh my goodness yes," Miss L'Hommedieu said warmly.

"It's just that it's been turned off," put in Gussie.

"Ever since Miss Thale—" It was Leo's voice, and they all turned to stare at him sharply. "—left us," he added lamely.

"Miss Thale?" Andrew was suddenly alert.

"We are her guests," explained Miss L'Hommedieu. "You haven't met her yet, she is away just now."

"Away?" Andrew echoed.

Miss L'Hommedieu picked up her spoon. "Since you have not met her, naturally she is away. Shall we eat now? Gussie's fish stews are delicious."

"Herbs in 'em," Leo volunteered. "Gussie raises 'em—eh, Gussie? Basil in this one, right?"

Tarragon said eagerly, "They have beautiful names, say them for him, won't you, Gussie?" In the candlelight her face had the translucence of a Renoir portrait.

Gussie nodded. "I'll tell a few, I don't mind. There's rosemary and summer savory, damask rose, lemon balm, sage, angelica—and tarragon."

"Tarragon!" exclaimed Andrew.

They all beamed at him, Tarragon looking the most pleased of all. "It was up to us to name her," explained Gussie, adding dryly, "Herbs grow very well in poor soil . . . Tarragon, 'there is nothing good or evil save in the will.' "

"Epictetus," said Tarragon.

"Leo?"

Leo gave Tarragon a stern glance and cleared his throat. " 'Inferiors revolt in order that they may be equal, and equals that they may be superior, and such is the state of mind which creates revolution.' " He did not wait for an answer but ducked his head again and applied himself to his soup.

"Aristotle," said Tarragon.

"She may not have had advantages, Mr. Oliver, but we've seen to it she's well read. Try her on something, go ahead."

Amused, Andrew said, " 'A man who knows he is a fool is not a great fool.' "

"Chuang Tzu," replied Tarragon, smiling.

Leo lifted his head, spoon in hand, to say, "What kind of work you do out there? You have a job?"

Startled, Andrew said, "Me? I work for Meredith Machines, writing copy for the company newsletter." *Courtesy of my father*, he thought bitterly.

"Like it?"

"No."

A rich chuckle emanated from the man. "Writing happy news to cheer up the poor bastards?"

"Now, Leo," Gussie said soothingly, and to Andrew, "He's a Marxist, you see."

"Workers of the world unite and all that?" quipped Andrew.

"And all that, yes," said Leo, glaring at him. "Going global aren't they—out there?"

Andrew, glancing around him, thought that "out there"

sounded just about right. "But how on earth do you know about global expansion—when it's out there, and you're here. And no electricity," he added.

"Radio," said Leo. "When we've batteries."

"No batteries?"

Leo shrugged. "At the moment, no. Anything new?"

Andrew considered this. "More wars . . . more revolutions . . . more mergers—even Meredith Machines."

"Ah, downsizing," murmured Leo. "Going to lose your job?"

"Probably not."

"Damn confident," responded Leo. "Know the boss?"

Andrew said weakly, "Well, yes. My father happens to be a vice president of the company."

"Hah," snorted Leo. "Nepotism."

Out of some irrational loyalty to his father, Andrew said angrily, "It's not my idea to work at Meredith Machines, it's simply that my father—surely this is natural—insists on my having a job with some income. Writing copy isn't creative, not compared to *real* writing—"

At the word *writing* Gussie broke in to say, "Miss L'Hommedieu writes. Show him, Miss L'Hommedieu. Read us what you wrote today, *please?*"

Miss L'Hommedieu said with dignity, "I much prefer my readings to take place evenings."

"Mr. Oliver may not be here," said Tarragon.

Gussie gave her a sharp glance but said only, "Do, Miss L'Hommedieu, you know how much we enjoy them."

"Oh very well." From among the layers of chiffon she drew out a sheet of paper, glanced at it, and cleared her throat. Once sure that she had everyone's attention she read, " 'The fires were burning late that night, small coins of brightness in the darkness. There were no drums, for the night could be full of ears, and what they planned must never be heard. If eyes watched from a distance they would see only four people speaking in low voices and solemnly nodding. Calmly, gravely, they discussed death . . . the death of Basil Hopkins French.' "

She stopped, folded up the sheet of paper, and restored it to an inner pocket.

Andrew, startled, said, "But that's *good*, what happens next?"

"I write only beginnings," said Miss L'Hommedieu.

"*Sometimes* endings," pointed out Tarragon.

"Yes, but not often. I find middles extremely dull."

"Yesterday's was ever so exciting," put in Tarragon. "About a woman named Marla Tempest who'd begun having very strange dreams."

Gussie said, "I preferred the one about the heartbroken young girl living near the ocean where she found a message in a bottle, washed in on a wave."

"And when she cleaned the bottle a genie came out," Tarragon told him with triumph.

Disconcerted, Andrew said, "Yes, but surely you want to know *more*? Want to know what happens *next*?"

"Why?" asked Miss L'Hommedieu.

Andrew realized that his mouth had dropped open in

astonishment as he groped for an answer. He said, "Because," and then he said, "Because—" and then he sensibly closed his mouth.

Gussie smiled forgivingly. "Now if everyone has finished their dinner it's nearing time to watch the sunset. You'll stay the night with us, Mr. Oliver? It's far too late to find a garage or a telephone."

He felt absurdly grateful for this offer, he had expected to sleep in his car. "Thank you, thank you very much," he told her.

"Then we'll retire to the porch now to see the sunset."

Impulsively he said, "What do you do when it rains?"

It was Leo who answered. "We watch the rain."

This left Andrew wondering why everything said here seemed to have a curious logic that struck him as indisputable and yet was scarcely logical at all. By now rather amused, Andrew followed them out to the porch, where he had first encountered Miss L'Hommedieu, and they all sat down to contemplate the sky. He had to admit that it was a very theatrical sunset, a combination of vivid pink, scarlet, and salmon, with a stripe of dull blue to introduce the coming night. He glanced at the faces beside him and found them intensely serious; Miss L'Hommedieu in particular looked ecstatic, almost embarrassingly so. On the other hand, he realized that he'd not noticed the setting of the sun in months and possibly years. In Manhattan the sun rose, the sun vanished, and was noted only when missing.

"There!" said Gussie abruptly as the brilliance vanished

behind the trees. "Tarragon, we've very little to entertain Mr. Oliver, it would be hospitable of you to show him the view from Bald Hill."

He said quickly, "Thank you, but I really must visit my car. I brought an overnight bag in the trunk, thinking I might be late returning to New York."

"Holding what?" demanded Leo.

Andrew said crisply, "Pajamas, toothbrush, swimsuit and towel, change of shirt."

This appeared to appease Leo. "Later," Gussie said with authority. "Tarragon—Bald Hill."

Bald Hill it would be, but since he was to be accompanied by Tarragon he made no further resistance. A *farmworker she must not marry,* he thought firmly, and perhaps he could explain to her the idiocy and the risks of an advertisement in the newspapers for a man. He followed her across the empty field and into the woods until the trees thinned and a very steep and cone-shaped hill presented itself—and bald it was, with not a tree on it. With a sigh he climbed the hill behind her, the only sound his quiet panting and the crunch of pebbles underfoot. He would have liked to stop and rest halfway up the hill, since it was steeper than he'd realized and he was out of condition, but Tarragon shamed him by going out of her way to climb joyfully over the occasional boulder rooted in the earth and then to proceed tirelessly toward the darkening sky at the summit. He was relieved when they reached the crest, and after catching his breath sat down on a rock to look.

The hill had brought them high above the mist that was stealing over Thale's Folly and was already settling in the valley below. From where they sat a group of smaller hills around them rose like islands out of a moving sea of cloud, and when the mist thinned, he could see dozens of twinkling lights, like stars, shining in a town somewhere below. New York seemed a thousand miles away. He said, "It's beautiful, it's like looking at the world upside down."

Tarragon turned and smiled at him. "I thought you'd like it."

He nodded. "I do, very much," but he was looking at her now, seated on the ground not far away and hugging her knees as she looked down into the valley. In the sky that had been filled with sunset, the moon was emerging now from behind clouds to shed a ghostly light, and in this play of light and shadow Tarragon's face was dark but the moonlight had turned her hair as pale as spun silver. "Tell me," he said. "Tell me how you ever came to live at Thale's Folly. You've been here a long time?"

"For as long as I can remember."

"That long?"

"Oh yes." Her smile deepened. "I think I'm rather like the others—someone nobody wanted."

He stared at her in astonishment. "What on earth makes you think that?"

She said cheerfully, "Because Miss Thale had the naming of me, and my birth certificate reads Tarragon Sage Valerian. I have the very strong suspicion that she found me abandoned on somebody's doorstep."

"Good heavens!" he exclaimed. "And named you *that*?"

She nodded. "Miss Thale was very into herbs, you know. She studied them, planted them, loved them." She laughed. "Of course when I was very little they told me that my mother was a beautiful heiress who eloped with a circus magician, after which both were killed falling from a tightrope . . . a little hard to believe, don't you think?"

He said cautiously, "It does sound rather exotic."

She nodded. "Gussie and Miss Thale collected people the way others collect stray cats. I mean *really* collected them; they'd drive around Pittsville once a week in their old Ford car looking for homeless people and people in trouble. When I was five or six there was a boy to play with—his name was Jake—and then an out-of-work Shakespearean actor—we called him Hamlet because he gave wonderful speeches from *Hamlet*—and a man who we called Merlin because he told fortunes, and there was Mr. Omelianuk who had only one leg, and Trudy who had run away from a husband who beat her, and a little girl named Jane. There have been all sorts of people staying with us, it's never been lonely."

And now you have me for a night, he thought, and hoped he wouldn't wake them with a nightmare. "But they've all left?"

"When they were ready to leave, yes."

"And you, are you ready to leave?" asked Andrew. "How old are you?"

"Nineteen."

"You don't *have* to be married at nineteen, you know, the idea's positively medieval." It suddenly seemed important to impress this upon her. *Very* important.

"I know that," she told him seriously, "it's just that it

would make them so happy to see me settled before"—she hesitated—"before Mr. Thale comes."

"Mr. Thale . . . Have I met him?" he asked innocently.

She shook her head. "You may not believe we could be so unscrupulous, Mr. Oliver, but nobody knows we're living here—except the mailman, of course, who brings Leo's checks each month. We could be found out at any moment. We'd like to believe Miss Thale is away visiting friends, but really she died five years ago and the farm belongs to her relatives now. They'd be ever so shocked to find us here."

"They would, yes," Andrew said truthfully.

"It's why they've advertised for a young man to fall in love with me."

"If he comes. If he falls in love."

"Oh, he will," she said confidently, "and then I need only select. That's very important, you know, to choose what's yours and reject what isn't. They've taught me *that*."

Amused, he said, "Such confidence!"

"Well, you see," she confided, "Gussie is very gifted, she knows how to cast magic spells." She added scornfully, "It's very rude when people call her a witch, but she does do wonders with our potatoes. We have to plant them at the dark of the moon and sprinkle ashes over them and—"

"Tarragon—"

"Mmmm?"

"For heaven's sake, there are no such things as magic spells and witches."

She laughed delightedly. "Then you'd be very unhappy if

you stayed long, Mr. Oliver. You should see our sunflowers, they're almost as high as the bean stalk in the fairy tale."

"The one that Jack climbed?"

"Yes."

He wanted to explain to her there was no such thing as magic, and that he was certainly proof of that. He wanted to tell her of the weeks—months now—that he'd moved through each day smiling and nodding, saying all the correct words, thinking too much and feeling nothing at all, but the moon had brightened the mist and was casting its own spell of enchantment over the hill, and the stars were coming out of hiding, and it was wonderfully restful, at least for the moment. He had never expected his mind and his nerves to be tranquilized and soothed by a moon, a star, a girl, and a treeless hill.

Tarragon said, "Shall we go back now?" When he didn't stir, she said, "You wanted to go to your car, didn't you? For pajamas?"

He sighed. He had no desire to move; he had even less desire to leave Bald Hill now that he'd arrived here. "Yes, we'd better go," he agreed, and relinquishing the rock on which he'd sat—or been glued, he thought wryly—he followed her out of the moonlight into the mist below, his sense of calm leaving him with every step. It would, as usual, be a sleeping-pill night.

 The mist had cleared when he set out on his mile-long return to the car. It was a lonely walk, and when the moon disappeared behind a cloud it was a dark one, enlivened only by the cheerful sound of crickets. When he reached the Mercedes, he was pleasantly surprised to find a flashlight in its compartment and regarded it with a new interest: *imagine*, he thought, *one need only press a button and there was light, no matches needed at all; a very remarkable invention*, he thought, *except for its need of batteries*. He remembered that Leo's radio needed batteries. Before he left Thale's Folly tomorrow he would make a point of buying a package of them for him, a fair exchange for those moments of peace on Bald Hill.

He shouldered his knapsack and headed back. Walking at a brisk pace—the flashlight helped—the trees lining the road seemed almost to be marching along with him, tall sentinels guarding the silent forest behind them that could—*might*, surely—be inhabited in this dark night by ghosts, a headless horseman, or—he thought with a smile—a witch who cast spells. Or possibly, as in Miss L'Hommedieu's story, he might find four people huddled around a campfire, planning the death of—what was his name—Basil Hopkins French? An owl suddenly broke the silence with a mournful hoot, the moon emerged again in the west from a bed of pale stars, and Andrew suddenly laughed aloud and couldn't think why.

Reaching Thale's Folly the house loomed black against the indigo-blue night sky, the turrets at each corner like twin exclamation marks. A solitary light shone in the kitchen window, *no doubt a kerosene lamp but more likely a candle*, he thought, and prayed the mattress they'd promised him for sleeping had not been chewed by squirrels or mice, because

in the morning he had a long walk ahead of him to find a telephone and a tow truck. Opening the door to the kitchen he
found Gussie waiting for him, and he was touched to see that
she'd brewed a cup of tea for him.

"Valerian—good for sleeping," she told him. "Bring it with
you, I'll show you to your room."

She led him up narrow carpeted stairs to the second floor,
and down the hall past closed doors. "Here," she said. "Miss
Thale's room." She handed him a candle, lighted it for him,
and was quite suddenly gone.

His candle sent shadows up and down across the ceiling;
he set it down on the old-fashioned oak stand and then sat on
the bed to drink his tea. His impression of the room was one
of ruffled white curtains at the windows, several ancient por-
traits, and a mirror on the wall and—oh, God, a chamber pot?
Gilt-edged, no less.

He could absorb no more; peeling off his clothes, he snuffed
out the candle, pulled on his pajamas, and as he sank down
into the bed he realized he'd not taken his sleeping pill.

Got to get up, he told himself . . . *have to . . . must get up . . .
must* . . . and was still mumbling when he fell asleep.

Sunday

3

If you have Pennyroyale in great quantity, dry and cast it into corrupt water, it helpeth it much, neither will it hurt them that drink thereof.　　　—John Gerard, *The Herball*, 1597

When Andrew awoke it was daylight and Miss L'Hommedieu was standing over his bed and staring down at him. He blinked at her, astonished.

She nodded. "I wanted to see what you looked like asleep. People are so interesting when asleep, don't you think?"

"No I don't," he said indignantly. "Are you going to watch me dress, too?"

But she was already floating out of the room, or gave that impression because this morning she was gowned in trailing blue chiffon that gave every appearance of bearing her away inside of it. "I've waited breakfast for you," she called from the hall.

He liked Miss L'Hommedieu, but he had little faith in the breakfast she was summoning him to. A glance out of the window assured him that the cacophony of birds outside indicated no crisis and that the sun was shining; he lingered a moment, captured by what he saw. No empty untilled field here: at the rear of the house the sun was shining down on a large and well-tended garden. Long mounded rows of earth, rich with leafy greens, stretched almost to the woods, with neat paths between each row, the far end shaded by a stand of knee-high corn, whose tassels shone like silk in the sun. As he buttoned up his shirt, he saw Leo emerge from somewhere below with a half-filled basket of ripe tomatoes. Passing the rows of lavish green he leaned over, picked a leaf, and chewing on it disappeared around the corner of the house. Andrew's years of summer camps had educated him about wells: there were two of them, with round cement lids encircled by bright flowers, and off to the left he could see a low circular stone wall that suggested a second, more sheltered garden. Standing at the window, he could already feel the heat of a July day; a hot walk lay ahead. He turned away and finished dressing.

Once downstairs he found his pessimism about breakfast justified: he was provided with a small glass of tomato juice, two slices of thin toast, and a cup of raspberry-leaf tea. Even as he pursued with a finger the last crumb of toast he managed to chat amiably with Miss L'Hommedieu about the weather until she suddenly held up a hand and said, "Hush! Something's coming!"

Something was indeed coming, and it sounded as if the house and the hills around them would be split asunder by the noise. Miss L'Hommedieu rose and went out to the porch with Andrew following. The noise grew shriller and more urgent, and then the cloud of dust that contained it swerved

into the driveway and bounced toward them. As the dust
cleared they saw a splendid chrome-and-scarlet motorcycle,
and astride it a figure in goggles, black leather jacket, black
trousers, and black boots.

The engine was shut off and the figure spoke. "Mmmmcha
Thale farm?"

"This is the Thale farm," Andrew told him.

Behind him the screen door opened, and Leo and Gussie
tiptoed out. The figure on the motorcycle moved. One leg
slid over the saddle, a hand swept back the Martian goggles,
and with the helmet removed they saw his face, round and
pudgy and oddly childlike, a sad contrast to his swashbuck-
ling arrival.

"S'wan of you Miss Gussie Pease?" he inquired, and am-
bled toward the porch, stopping with one booted foot on the
step. "Mm looking for a job, muh name's Wally Blore."

"Well!" said Gussie with feeling. "We're delighted to see
you, Mr. Blore. Won't you come in and have a cup of tea? Tarragon will make the tea, we'd love to have you meet Tarragon,
too."

Andrew became aware of Miss L'Hommedieu elbowing him
sharply in the ribs. "Should we be alarmed?" she whispered.
"Are we being invaded? Ask him if he speaks any English."

He turned and smiled at her; he had not realized how fond
of her he was becoming. "It's going to be all right," he told
her. "Trust Gussie until I get back. I don't know why," he
added reflectively, "but she can't marry Tarragon off in just
one morning." He had a sudden vision of Blore encountering
Tarragon and a premonition that he would whistle when he

met her. He turned away, and picking up his car keys strode angrily down the road to find rescue for the car.

It was midafternoon before Andrew limped back to Thale's Folly, a little wiser in country mores and a little humbler. He had met the postmaster, whose name was Artemus and who was tending the grocery counter at the post office while his wife was at church.

"Groceries! In a post office?" Andrew was surprised.

"Wife's idea," confided Artemus. "Woods full of summer cottages and artists, saves them a trip to town and gives my wife pin money. All we had once along that wall"—he pointed to the shelves of groceries—"was a lot of WANTED pictures. Killers, all of them—very dispiriting. Wife's idea," he replied.

"And a very good one," said Andrew, and at once bought six jelly doughnuts and consumed three of them while Artemus commiserated with him; it had been a long walk on two slices of toast and a cup of tea.

"Trouble is," Artemus said, fixing him with a piercing eye, "it's Sunday and you're not going to get anyone from town to drive out on a Sunday. Manuel's got a tow truck; I'll give him a ring, he should be back from Mass by now."

Manuel, it seemed, belonged to the garage—closed—that he'd passed yesterday.

Calls were made; Manuel had just returned from Mass, he would need to change his clothes and rev up his tow truck— "probably have lunch, too," Artemus said—and be there inside of an hour.

Haunted by his meager breakfast, Andrew considered what

he might take back with him to Thale's Folly. Radio batteries, of course, for Leo. Bread they seemed already to have. "I'll take a dozen eggs," he told Artemus, and then realized that no electricity meant no refrigerator. "Make it six eggs," he said, and then, "No, damn it, make it a dozen." He tried to think of what they didn't grow in the garden; no use flaunting his money, and a long way to carry whatever he bought. "And ten of those chocolate bars," he added, and thought, *God I've been spoiled.*

Manuel, when he arrived, shook his head over Andrew's situation. "That's a killer of a road," he said. "Has potholes there big enough to bury a cow. Hop in."

Andrew said good-bye to Artemus and obligingly climbed up into the tow truck.

"You at the motel?" asked Manuel.

Andrew hesitated before saying, "No. No, I kept walking, hoping for a house with a phone, and there was a house—"

Manuel nodded. "A house."

"Yes. They put me up for the night. You know them?"

Manuel only shrugged. "Heard tell."

"Interesting group of people."

This met with no response. "Here we are," Manuel said, and braked at the site of Andrew's disaster.

The car was inspected, the pothole assessed, and the news was not good. "What you got," said Manuel, hands on hips and scowling, "is a hole in the muffler. You've also lost your tailpipe, and this tire's been torn up pretty bad."

Andrew nodded.

"Tailpipe and muffler I got," Manuel continued, "but this here tire—" He shook his head. "Have to order one from town. Take a day, maybe two."

Andrew found himself relieved by this news and decided that his pleasure probably equaled the anger his father would soon feel; he might not be concerned about Andrew, but definitely he would be concerned—no, he would be furious—about the company car. Because of this, once Manuel had hitched the Mercedes to his truck, Andrew rode back with him to the post office and left a message with his father's answering service. Only then did he begin his walk back again to Thale's Folly, which felt a long walk this time and gave him too much time to think. Once, an eternity ago, or so it felt, he had been considered brilliant to have had two well-received mystery novels published by the age of twenty-five. The fact that he could no longer write, was utterly blocked and was unable to summon even the slightest interest in it now did not preclude his thinking, observing, and living with words, so that as he walked up Thale Road he was as usual searching for words to describe Artemus: white hair worn long in the back—could he have come to Tottsville as a hippie when younger? Comfortable-looking man. Laid-back. Sleepy eyes. Striking black brows untouched by white. Manuel? Burly and broad-shouldered, shrewd eyes—would his bill be huge?— not a talker—large, capable hands.

Mere note-taking, he thought bitterly, he couldn't even do as well as Miss L'Hommedieu. What did the dictionary say about trauma? *A disordered psychic or behavioral state resulting from mental or emotional stress or physical injury.* Such helplessness—such estrangement—infuriated him, and since his anger so often led to depression, he was growing accustomed to hating himself. He was still hating himself when he turned into the driveway of Thale's Folly and Tarragon ran to meet him.

"You've walked!" she cried happily. "No car? You're not leaving yet?"

At once Andrew stopped hating himself, touched by her eagerness and her delight in seeing him. It occurred to him how different she was from girls he'd known: Jennifer, for instance, with her artificial bronze tan and bright carmine lipsticks, whose greeting would have been cool and guarded in comparison. Tarragon's bleached and shabby jeans and sweatshirt matched the blue of her eyes and the blue of the sky, and as for her cheekbones, *a model would kill for them,* he thought. "The car's at the garage," he said. "I can't leave. Manuel says it may take another day, probably two for repairs."

"I'm so glad," she said, and they stood in the driveway smiling at each other.

He said at last, awkwardly, "I've brought eggs. And batteries for Leo, too."

"That's kind of you," she said. "What's even nicer is that there's not going to be a moon tonight—you can see how it's clouding over now—and Leo says you can go with us. It's dump night."

Puzzled, he said, "Dump night? You mean like bingo night? What dump?"

"The town dump. It's not far from here, and it's a wonderful place for treasure."

He asked with interest, "And why is it necessary to go at the dark of the moon?"

They began walking toward the house and he waited, braced. "Well, you see," she explained, "it's illegal."

He nodded. "Of course—I don't know why I asked."

"Hobe Elkins lives there in a shack, you see, and he's posted NO DUMP PICKING UNDER PENALTY OF FINES and NO TRESPASS- ING signs. Leo says tonight is perfect for it because there's a kerosene-burning space heater there. He saw it."

Amused, Andrew said, "And what will you do with a kerosene space heater, whatever it is?"

"Do with it?" She gave him an astonished glance. "Why, keep warm with it. If we shut off the upstairs next winter it will heat most of the downstairs."

"Your furnace, I suppose . . . ?"

She nodded. "In February. The boiler cracked . . . Oh, do let's go in so you can tell Gussie about the eggs, she makes wonderful sorrel omelettes and she'll be so pleased, and Wally Blore left early for a motorcycle meet so you can have the mint tea Gussie made for him."

Gussie's eyes brightened at being presented with a dozen eggs, and she promised a sorrel omelette. Leo's gratitude at sight of the batteries was so shyly touching that Andrew felt downright heroic. At once Leo headed upstairs for his radio, calling over his shoulder, "There may be news about the Pittsville bank robbery last week, I missed all the excitement about *that*." He sounded so gleeful that he left Andrew won- dering, given Leo's anarchist approach to life, just where his sympathies might lie in the case of such a raid on a bank.

Gussie's sorrel omelette was exquisite; Leo sadly reported no news of the robbery on the local radio station; and Miss L'Hommedieu, perhaps aware of the pervading excitement over dump night, had produced only a few lines of a story and announced that she preferred to complete it before sharing it.

What no one had explained to Andrew was that Leo embraced such expeditions with the ardor of a military commander; Leo had unsuspected depths. It was nearly midnight when they crept from the house—crept, thought Andrew, being the only way to describe their exit—and he decided they resembled nothing so much as Halloweeners going out to trick-or-treat. Masquerades had always embarrassed Andrew, and he was embarrassed now, for Tarragon had pinned him into a dark blanket that was supposed to make him invisible. What was even more humiliating, Gussie had daubed his face with mud and he had been placed in charge of a homemade wagon in which they would carry off the loot: he felt like a commando wheeling a baby carriage. Leo had been right about no moon, but he had refused Andrew's flashlight—"on a mission like this?" said Leo in a shocked voice—and so they stumbled and tripped down the road in this moonless night until Leo abruptly halted them.

"Dump's a quarter of a mile in," he whispered, pointing, and they left the road behind them to follow a narrow path through the woods. Halting them again he said, "Tarragon, you're reconnaissance, we get closer you check Hobe's position and movements. Andrew, you're to review the terrain for holes, booby traps and mines."

"Mines?" said Andrew incredulously.

"Enemy may have been alerted." Leo's voice was contemptuous.

They moved forward again over what was extremely rough ground until the balmy night turned smoky and disagreeable and Andrew saw a flickering half-light through the trees up ahead. Their stealthy pace continued until the trees were behind them and they stood at the edge of the dump.

Dante's hell, thought Andrew, for there were no visible flames but from the far corner of the clearing there emanated a weird red glow, as if a subterranean furnace had been banked for the night.

"Tarragon?" whispered Leo.

"Right," responded Tarragon, and left them to reconnoiter. A few minutes later she was back. "All quiet. He must be sound asleep."

"My turn now?" asked Andrew dryly.

"Roger. Stove over there," said Leo, pointing to a mountain of tins. "Hobe's shack is back of it. Signal with flares when safe for advance." He handed Andrew two kitchen matches.

Andrew said indignantly, "I don't suppose we could just walk over and load the blasted thing on this baby carriage? Oh never mind," he added, and to appease Leo—he had never felt more ridiculous—he began an impressively cautious approach, zigging and zagging, stopping to listen and then zigzagging again.

He nearly fell over the heater. He swore, regained his balance, and brought one of the kitchen matches from his pocket and lighted it by ripping it across the shutter of the stove.

To his surprise the striking of the match across the stove precipitated a snakelike hissing noise and something zoomed past Andrew's ear to shoot skyward and light up the dump as if day had arrived. Stepping back in astonishment he tripped and fell and a tin can hit him squarely on the head. As he staggered to his feet a rocket discharged into the sky a nearly perfect red white and blue American flag that hung over him for a moment, blindingly brilliant until its stars melted into the night.

"All right, buster," snarled the man standing over Andrew. "Into my shack. *Move!*"

"What the devil," gasped Andrew. "Look here—"

"Faster," growled the man, and he was actually waving a gun. A shocked Andrew moved with consummate speed, pushed and driven to the door of the shack; the door was slammed behind them, and Andrew shoved roughly against a wall in the corner. At once he slid to the floor to become as inconspicuous as possible because Hobe Elkins appeared to be a man demented. In the darkness it was difficult to guess what was happening but he could hear Elkins stamping around the room, kicking walls and shouting, "Take that, you bastard—and *that*! Teach you to come here to my dump, teach you to stop trespassing, hit you again I will." More walls were kicked and thumped and then abruptly the shouting stopped and there was silence.

"I think they've got it," Elkins whispered.

"Got what?" asked Andrew weakly.

"It's all right, they've got it," he said again. He struck a match, ran up the wick of a kerosene lamp and lighted it, and the sudden brightness showed a calm and smiling man. "It's all right, they're gone," he said, beaming at Andrew.

Bewildered, Andrew nodded toward the door. "You mean you let them take that blasted heater?"

Elkins chuckled. "You can't say I didn't give 'em a run for their money. You tripped a wire back there soon as you touched the heater. Took me darn near a day getting that rigged up." He gleefully slapped his thigh.

Andrew sat up, staring. "You mean you don't *mind* their taking the heater?"

"Mind! I've had it parked out there for a week where Leo could see it. Their furnace broke down last winter, you know, can't let 'em freeze to death." He glanced at Andrew and shook his head. "Beats me the way they just ran off and left you like this."

"I'm expendable," Andrew said gloomily, "I'm over twenty."

"Not to worry, they'll be back, it'll come to them I've beaten you up—give 'em something to talk about for weeks. It'll be an adventure for Leo, rescuing you. You imbibe, mister?"

"Imbibe?" Andrew said cautiously. "I think I could use a little *something*. I don't want to complain but this evening has been a trifle hard on the nerves."

"Got just the thing!" Elkins brought a jug from under his bed. "Don't often have someone to drink with . . . Blackberry brandy," he explained happily. "One hundred proof. Ought to know, made it myself."

Time passed until dimly, through a haze of imbibed brandy, Andrew became aware that he was lying on a rough and splintery floor and there were voices: He heard Tarragon cry, "Mr. Elkins, you've nearly killed him, he's unconscious!" Leo shouted, "You brute, you ought to be shot for this!" and Andrew smiled contentedly. He was lifted from the floor, wheels began turning under him, and somewhere up ahead a lamp shone in the darkness. After a great many jarrings and bumps Leo spoke again. "Treat him gently, Gussie, he was a real hero." With effort someone propelled him upstairs to a bed, and Andrew gratefully fell across it.

A voice said, "And did you have a pleasant chat with Hobe Elkins?"

Andrew opened one eye and saw that Gussie was tucking him into bed. There was no one else in the room.

"Chat?" he echoed. "*Chat?* He did terrible things to me! If you'd been there—he's a wild man!"

"Torture, Mr. Oliver?"

"Of the worst kind!"

She said dryly, "Strange . . . it smelled to me exactly like blackberry brandy."

He opened both eyes now and found her over by the doorway holding up a candle and smiling at him. She said gently, "You needn't pretend with me, Mr. Oliver. Hobe is a truly charitable man, he never embarrasses us by giving gifts, he allows us to steal them from him, which makes his charity bearable. Good night, Mr. Oliver."

Startled, Andrew said, "Good night."

She lingered a moment, regarding him with compassion. "You will, of course, feel miserable in the morning, Mr. Oliver, but if you can manage to reach the kitchen, I have something that will mend the damage. Sleep well . . ."

But Andrew was already asleep.

Monday

4

Houndes Tongue will tye the tongues of Houndes so that
they shall not bark at you, if it be laid under the bottom of
your feet.   —John Gerard, *The Herball*, 1597

When Andrew awoke it was to an achingly bright and
sunny room with a concert of birds chattering in the
tree beyond the window. *Dump night*, he remembered . . .
Hobe Elkins . . . and he groaned, felt his head—it had not
floated away, after all—and edging himself into a sitting position he waited for the thunder to subside while the birds continued to annoyingly, cheerfully, and reproachfully upbraid
him. Hazily he remembered Gussie promising something to
make him fit again; relieved to find that he was still in his
clothes he placed one foot gingerly on the floor, then the
other, and slowly stood up. Feeling a hundred years old he
made his way cautiously down the hall and step-by-step down
the stairs, clinging to the railing.

At the kitchen table Tarragon was shelling peas and looked
up to give him a mischievous grin. Gussie brought him a glass
of juice. "Freshly squeezed tomato with a mix of herbs and a

smidgen of—I'd better not say. Drink it down," she said sternly. "Fast. No nonsense. *Drink.*"

Andrew drank, sputtering, choking, his throat burning and gasped, "Good God, liquid *fire?* What's in it, horseradish, cayenne pepper?"

Gussie only smiled.

Whatever its contents, it proved a powerful enough antidote to remind him of his purpose in coming to Thale's Folly. Already it was Monday, and past midmorning, and he'd not inspected these twenty-five acres for his father or taken pictures of them. Admittedly the ambience of Thale's Folly was not conducive to the minutiae of data-collecting, but it had to be done, hangover or not. Accepting a slice of toast he announced that he would take a walk to further clear his head, and fetching his knapsack—he didn't want them to see maps, deed, and camera—he walked out into a sweetly fragrant morning. In the untilled field across from the porch Wally Blore was leaning on his spade, with few signs of the earth having been turned over, and *He won't last long*, thought Andrew, cheered by the thought.

He walked past the garden in the rear and found the path that he assumed must lead to the pond or brook where Tarragon had caught her fish. It was a narrow path, well worn by use, and he'd left the house behind him when he was startled to hear the thud of feet ahead of him, and of someone breathing heavily—he'd not expected foot traffic—and suddenly Manuel appeared around the curve in the path, bare-chested and wearing neon-bright red shorts.

Breathlessly he fluttered a hand at Andrew and stopped. "Lunch hour—jogging," he panted. "Came by the shortcut. Something thought you should know."

Andrew winced. "Car's in worse shape than you thought?"

Manuel shook his head. "Not that. Somebody stopped at the garage this morning. Not wanted by the police, are you?"

Indignantly Andrew said, "Of course not!"

Manuel nodded, and Andrew was relieved to see that his breathing was returning to normal. "Seemed mighty interested in your car. Looked it over, asked questions about you, like where and who you are."

"That's rather strange," Andrew said. "Who would know I'm here? What did you tell him? Or her?"

"Him," said Manuel. "Told him none of his business, repairing cars is *my* business." He grinned. "Except I wasn't that polite."

"What did he look like?"

"City fellow."

"Thin? Fat? Tall? Short? Business suit?"

"Thin. Tan raincoat. Suit. Rolex watch. Not tall, not short. Black hair."

Puzzled, Andrew said, "Doesn't sound like anyone I'd know."

"And maybe somebody you'd not want to know, Mr. Oliver. Didn't much like the look of him, frankly. *Or* his attitude. Pushy. I got instincts about people, you know?"

Since Andrew had instincts about people, too, he didn't question this. "It's a mystery to me, think he'll come back?"

"Could," said Manuel. "Might. Will if he wants to keep

an eye on your car. Considering his interest . . . Depends, don't it?"

"Definitely it depends," agreed Andrew, "but definitely it's weird. Thanks for telling me."

Manuel nodded, and having delivered his message he turned, surveyed the path by which he'd arrived, sighed, took a long deep breath and set out again, his bare legs flashing white against the shadows ahead. Andrew, following slowly, listened to the sound of his receding footsteps, and to the return of that country stillness that was still somewhat unnerving to him. He was touched by Manuel's neighborliness, realized too late that he should have asked him about that shortcut, and wondered who on earth could be so interested in Meredith Machines' company car. A mistake, he decided . . . big mistake, it had to be. In the meantime there was the pond or brook to find and at least twenty more acres to explore. He glanced to his right and thought, *My God, the trees are thick in these woods, it's like twilight in there*, and he was aware of a sudden and inexplicable impulse to learn what lay beyond the path in that twilit world.

He peered curiously into and through the screen of sumac. A small breeze had found its way to the path and the leaves of the trees lining it danced fitfully, twisting and turning, quite unlike their neighboring conifers whose plump well-furnished bodies only swayed with matronly dignity, but inside the forest, deep in the woods, there was only stillness, no movement, and without wind the leaves hung limp. Deeper yet a fallen tree lay across the forest floor, bleached a silvery-white, and beyond this, in the distance, he saw that sunlight had found its way through the tapestry of leaves to plant its brilliance on green moss and etch the leaves bright green.

He realized that he was not only curious but interested, and he'd felt neither for a long time; he wanted to enter the woods and find that sunlit expanse of emerald green and yet he felt paralyzed by dread.

It would be very still in there, he realized.

Frighteningly still.

I might have to face myself, he thought.

He took one step forward and then another. Breaking through the scrub and sumac at the path's edge he made his way around and over lichen-covered rocks and boulders until he was in among the tightly knit trees. Dried twigs snapped underfoot; last autumn's yellowed leaves made a damp bed for evil-looking mushrooms and patches of sickly white flowers. A squirrel ran up a tree and a bird flew away in alarm at his passage. Reaching the sward of green at last, brilliant emerald in the sun, he stopped in surprise. "What on earth!" he exclaimed, and at the sound of his voice a small creature, rabbit or mouse, scurried across the moss and out of sight among the trees.

What he was seeing was: a perfect circle of stones occupying half of this soft green carpet of moss, a low stone table on which was arranged a candle, a bowl, a cup, a long stick, and a bell. An old iron cauldron stood in its center and beside it, on the other side, another candle, a bowl, the design of a pentacle drawn in blue chalk, a cup . . . He said again, "What on earth!"

Behind him a voice said sternly, "You shouldn't be here, this is *private*."

It was Tarragon.

"But what *is* this?" he asked. "Damned if it doesn't look like some kind of altar."

"And you shouldn't *be* here," she said accusingly.

"Well, I *am* here and it does look to me like an altar."

She said impatiently, "Of course it is. I *told* you, on Bald Hill, about Gussie. I kept no secrets."

"You didn't tell me she was a *real* witch, a *practicing* witch."

"And you"—she flung at him—"didn't tell me your name is Thale."

This silenced him, and he stood very still.

"There's a man back at the house," she told him coldly. "A Mr. Selkirk. He's looking for an Andrew Thale, he drove up from New York this morning looking for him. That's you, isn't it? You're not Andrew Oliver at all."

Damn his father, he thought. He said stiffly, "The answer to that is yes and no. That is, my name is Andrew *Oliver* Thale, and my father sent me, except he told me the house was empty and had been empty for years, and when it wasn't—"

"How cowardly," she said bitingly. "Telling lies like that."

"Cowardly? *Cowardly?*" he repeated. "When I found you and Gussie and Miss L'Hommedieu and Leo living here? and *happily?*"

"And are we to be turned out of the house now?"

"There's no buyer," he told her. "Really there isn't. He just wanted to know—"

She nodded. "Its value."

They regarded each other steadily for a long moment, and then she turned away and he followed her around the circle of stones into a path new to him; they walked in silence until they emerged at the edge of the empty field near the porch, where Wally Blore was again leaning on his spade but quickly began to dig at sight of them.

"I think Wally has got to *go*," said Tarragon.

"So another potential husband can replace him?" He hoped he didn't sound spiteful.

With a wicked smile she said, "If I could *only* persuade Gussie to do some *incantations* at the next full moon and cast her *magic spells* again, I'm sure that someone *much* nicer will show up."

"Hah!" he said scornfully, and as they approached the house he braced himself next for Mr. Selkirk. It would have to be Selkirk, of course, because he was a lower-management man who was often assigned his father's dirty work—*when I'm not assigned it*, thought Andrew. There was no sign of a car, and they found the man seated at the kitchen table over a cup of tea with Leo, Gussie, and Miss L'Hommedieu.

Selkirk rose when Andrew entered—after all, Andrew was the son of a VP—and said, "Good morning, Andrew. Your father's sent me to bring you back. The company car can be returned later."

Andrew said crossly, "I didn't see your car outside. Resting in a pothole?"

"Oh, I could see *that* would never do," Selkirk said smugly.

"I walked in from the highway, and now that you're here, Andrew, we'd better get started back to New York."

"So you're a Thale," Gussie said pleasantly. "I thought there was something familiar about you."

Andrew reminded himself to ask if there was a picture of Great-Aunt Harriet in the house, but at the moment he had other business at hand. "I'm not going back," he told Selkirk. "My father asked for a report and there's no report yet."

"But this is Monday!" protested Selkirk. "A working day!"

"And I am working," pointed out Andrew.

Leo interrupted to point an accusing finger at Selkirk. "Can't believe what I've been hearing! Bloody corporate business, Andrew, this man tells me six thousand people getting fired at your bloody Meredith place. Excess, he calls it. Redundancy."

Andrew was startled. "I heard four thousand."

"Four thousand at Meredith Machines," said Selkirk, "two thousand at PGH Plastics."

"Mergers," sniffed Leo. "Cutting costs and getting rid of excess, he says. Why can't he say the word *people*? It sticks in your throat, doesn't it, Selkirk? Tossed out like garbage. In my day—"

Miss L'Hommedieu gently interrupted him. "Leo, I was about to read my new story. Yesterday's story."

"Oh," said Leo penitently. "Sorry, Miss L'Hommedieu."

It occurred to Andrew that no one ever called Miss L'Hommedieu by her first name.

Miss L'Hommedieu cleared her throat, held up her page of written words to the light, and began: " 'The girl, Suzanne,' " she read, " 'was browsing in the St. John's Thrift Shop with an eye for something Victorian that could be worn in *Lady Windermere's Fan*, a play in which she had a minor part . . . Seeing a velvet jacket, she carried it to a mirror and then removed her own jacket to try it on. It did not fit sleekly, due to a slight bulge in one side, and she saw that something had long ago been taped between two seams. Making sure that no one saw her she carefully applied herself to tearing away the worn tape and found a slip of yellowed paper, which she unfolded. It was a map, clumsily drawn and very old, with an X in faded red and the words BURIED GOLD HERE 1896, 20 MILES SW KAFUE.' "

She stopped, and Mr. Selkirk said, "Go on, what next? Don't stop!"

Andrew smiled at him benevolently. "She doesn't write middles. Hadn't you better be starting back to New York?"

Selkirk wrenched his gaze from Miss L'Hommedieu and turned to Andrew. "And just what do I tell your father?"

"That I've not been able to complete a report yet, and I'm not coming back with you."

"Good for you," cheered Leo.

"You're a very promising young man," said Miss L'Hommedieu graciously.

"And obviously forgiven for being a Thale," pointed out Tarragon, looking amused.

Mr. Selkirk rose from the table reluctantly. "Your father's not going to like this, Andrew."

"It can scarcely upset him when it's he who sent me here."

"He won't like it," he repeated. "You know your father."

"Only too well," said Andrew.

"Which means a long walk back to my car for me, and a long drive back to Manhattan." He sighed heavily. "Waste, waste," and with the melancholy of a martyr he thanked them for the tea and left.

His departure was followed by a long silence. Andrew dared not speak, and no one looked at him.

Tarragon said, "He just wanted a report, there's no buyer, Gussie."

"Yet," growled Leo.

"I hope I'm not impertinent," said Andrew, "but why did Miss Thale leave this property to my father—she couldn't have given a damn about him, excusing my language—and not to you?"

"She never made a will," Gussie said in a gruff voice. "Fit as a fiddle she was—"

"—and then keeled over in the garden picking chives," added Leo.

"So as next of kin the property automatically went to my father . . . ? I'm sorry," Andrew said. "Really sorry."

Leo nodded. "And the property goes to a vice president already rich as Croesus."

"No," Andrew said, considering this, "my father's not *rich* rich. He started out with nothing—with a bicycle repair shop, actually, it's just that he's terrifyingly ambitious. It's true that he makes an incredible amount of money now, enough to have sent me to private schools and summer camps, but I worked my way through college—well, two years of it, anyway, before I quit to—to"—with a glance at Miss L'Hommedieu he hesitated and out of courtesy said instead—"to do what I wanted to do, which has given me a small income of my own, not much now but enough, at least it *was* enough until—until—" He stopped, his voice unsteady.

Tarragon said quickly, "If you're here to make a report for your father you'd better start, hadn't you?" To Gussie she said, "I'll make sandwiches and show him the pond."

Stationing herself at the counter she sliced bread and then reached for two apples and sliced them as well.

"*Apple* sandwiches?" said Andrew, startled.

"Yes, from the root cellar," Tarragon explained.

Once again Andrew reproached himself for expecting the predictable. "Of course," he said, and arming himself with his camera and carrying the jug of water and food, the two of them walked out into the heat of the afternoon.

They passed the garden and entered the narrow twisting path he'd taken earlier, where the drowsy July heat mingled the scents of warm earth, pine needles, and wildflowers. From the grass on either side sprang daisies, black-eyed Susans, and buttercups, and Tarragon stopped to lean over and pick a white flower that rose high above the daisies. "Yarrow," she said. "*Achillea millefolium.*"

"You're showing off," he told her.

"Yes, but aren't you impressed?"

Off on their right the thick woods had retreated to form a more distant dark wall, separated from them now by a belt of sunny scrub and a few stands of birches. From behind one of those birches Andrew saw a plume of smoke rising, and stopped in alarm.

"Fire!" he gasped. "Tarragon, smell the smoke? Dangerous!" Abandoning her, he rushed through the grass to save them all from disaster. Reaching the tree that concealed the flames he peered around it and shouted indignantly, "Hey!"

A man squatted behind the tree, paying no heed at all to Andrew's shout. Andrew couldn't see his face, only an unkempt head of stringy white hair and a shabby old coat, much mended and full of pockets. The man had built a small fire efficiently surrounded by stones, and from a tripod made out of a wire clothes hanger there hung a small pan of water that was beginning to steam. As Andrew watched, the man drew from a pocket two white eggs and lovingly, gently, lowered them into the boiling water. From another pocket he extracted a chocolate bar, broke it into quarters, returned three to another pocket, and began to eat it solemnly.

Andrew couldn't identify the egg but very definitely the chocolate bar matched those he'd brought to Thale's Folly from the post office.

"It's all right," Tarragon said, joining him. "That's Mr. Branowski, he doesn't hear you because he's deaf."

Andrew said grimly, "I *thought* the omelette last night was a bit skimpy. You know him, then . . ."

"Oh yes, Mr. Branowski—he's very shy—passes through every July. It was a long time before we knew he was here. One year he had pneumonia and Miss Thale and Gussie nursed him back to health and we've been friends ever since, but Gussie didn't tell me he's back."

Removing a burr from his jeans he followed her back to the path. "And you feed him."

She turned to look at him, wide-eyed. "But of course we feed him!" Very seriously she added, "Leo once read us the loveliest words that Rousseau wrote, I don't know where. He wrote 'What wisdom can you find that is greater than kindness?'. . . Isn't that lovely?"

"Very," he acknowledged, "but a scarce commodity these days."

"And there's the pond," she told him, as if presenting him with a gift.

It was a surprisingly large pond, rimmed with forest except for the shore opposite where they stood, and he realized the several cottages occupying that shore must be those he'd glimpsed from the highway: Bide-A-Wee, Rest-A-Wile, and Sunset Roost, each with lawns running down to the water that glittered in the afternoon sun. "No boats?" he said.

She laughed. "Where would they go? There's a brook feeding the pond off there"—she pointed—"and an outlet over there. For fishing, Leo's patched an old rubber raft we hide behind the bushes. And there's good swimming, and Miss Thale stocked it with trout, and there's a net at the outlet to keep them from swimming away from us so they multiply and have families."

"Are those cottages part of the property?" he asked.

"No, only this side." She jumped down to a shallow beach of pebbles and he joined her. "The property line runs through the middle of the pond, technically, because there was no pond here at all until Miss Thale dammed up the brook. And this is *my* rock," she told him, inviting him to sit with her at the very edge of the water. "Miss Thale was very firm about leaving a few big rocks to sit on."

But he remained standing with the water lapping at his feet. The pond was dazzling in the sunshine and a warm breeze ruffled the surface of the water, sending minuscule waves to lap at the rock on which Tarragon sat. A school of minnows darted away below him, and blades of drowned grass swayed languidly with the movement of each wave. It was another moment of peace and he was grateful.

He was not to enjoy it. Tarragon said in a matter-of-fact voice, not looking at him, "You screamed several times in your sleep last night. You seemed to think you were in an airplane."

So he'd screamed. *Damn*, he thought. Humiliating. Downright embarrassing. "I'm sorry," he said. "Sorry you heard it. I'm recovering from what you might call"—he winced—"all right, a nervous breakdown."

Pouring water from the jug into two cups she said companionably, "What causes that sort of thing?"

He was accustomed to saying that he preferred not to talk about it, but everything about Tarragon was so artless, so natural and different, that he found himself saying, "I let a friend persuade me to fly with him in his single-engine, one-prop plane . . . I'd never flown in such a small plane, there was only this thin sheath of metal between me and the earth below; I kept looking for something to hang on to, to keep from falling out, which seems ironic, considering . . . I remember Burke saying we were flying at five thousand feet and would I like to try nine thousand feet and I shouted, 'Please NO!'" which may have been what saved us, because a few minutes later the engine went dead, the propeller stopped turning, and down we went." He hesitated and then, "It felt a very long time, that fall to earth—an illusion, of course, but that's what I have nightmares about, watching the earth come closer and closer, and the plane in free fall. Expecting—waiting—to be smashed and dead in a few seconds."

"But it didn't happen."

"No," he said. "Burke had been sweating over whatever steers the damn thing, and he managed to lift the nose of the plane just enough to catch the wind, so instead of plunging straight down we crashed flat-out into the side of a hill." He shivered, remembering. "The next suspense was getting out in case the plane should explode, and with both of us badly hurt. We crawled out and it *did* explode," he added grimly, "which at least brought help fast. The noise and the flames."

"It sounds *dreadful*," she said. "And badly hurt!"

He shrugged. "Concussion, two broken ribs, bruises, shock, a broken leg. But we both survived." He sighed. "They tell me I healed quickly, being young—physically, at least—but there's no way to heal shattered nerves from the terror of it . . . In my sleep I keep falling out of the sky."

"Like Icarus," she said gravely, and considered it thoughtfully. "It's a strange expression, a breakdown of nerves. What do nerves look like, I wonder." Frowning, she held up the flower that she'd picked on their walk to the pond, and curling her fingers around it she crushed it. "I have just shattered this yarrow *cruelly*," she said. "Would it feel like that?"

She *did* understand. "Somewhat, yes. It's certainly tiresome and depressing. I don't sleep well, for one thing, but worst of all it's left me unable to write."

"Write?"

"Yes. In that other life—before it happened—I'd written two published books." He hesitated and then, with a wry smile, "They both seem pretty frivolous to me right now, but it's all I've ever wanted to do. I was writing stories when I was nine years old—very bad ones, but I *had* to write. If I can't do that anymore it really scares me. Shock, the doctor calls it, but it doesn't go away, everything seems meaningless and futile, I no longer *feel* anything."

"That must be *very* troubling," she said, absently handing him a sandwich. "Miss L'Hommedieu writes, you know. She says she makes up stories because she doesn't like reality."

Diverted, he said, "But her stories have neither middles nor endings."

"Perhaps," Tarragon said thoughtfully, "perhaps her life has been like that. All beginning, and no proper middle." She leaned over, picked up a stone, and tossed it into the water. "I've often wondered about that."

"Don't you ask?" he said, watching the widening circles that her stone drew on the water's surface.

"Oh no," she said, "we'd never ask, it wouldn't be fair. She's another of Miss Thale's strays and that was one of Miss Thale's rules: no questions. Because those who come here are—well, survivors."

"Of what?"

She looked suddenly mischievous. "Of nervous breakdowns?"

He laughed in spite of himself. "So I've wandered into the right place, you think?"

"No—were *sent* here," and with a quick demure glance at him she said, "but I think you *must* stay awhile, at least until the gypsies come."

"Gypsies!"

"Yes, they always come in July on their way north, about the time when Mr. Branowski arrives."

"And what will gypsies do for my nightmares?" he asked. "Or are you thinking of magic incantations from Gussie?"

"I don't think you understand Wicca, Mr. Thale," she said sternly. "Incantations are really *prayers*."

"Until now you called me Andrew," he pointed out.

"Yes, but you just turned into a Mr. Thale," she retorted.

"Touché," he said, and bit into his sandwich. "This isn't as much of a shock as I thought, once one adjusts to eating a fruit sandwich."

"Dandelion leaves make delicious sandwiches, too," she confided. "Although only in the spring, of course, when they're fresh. Incidentally, you've not taken a snapshot of the lake yet for your father."

With his mouth full of sandwich he picked up his camera and snapped a picture. "There, it's done."

Amused, she said, "You don't seem to really like your father."

"We're allergic to each other," he said ruefully, putting away his camera. "I've been a great disappointment to him because I'm not mechanical. When I was a kid he'd give me toy machines, and things to take apart and put together, but all I did was sketch, draw cartoons and make up stories. It's been a real shock to him that I've not followed in his foot-steps. Very puzzling for him, actually."

"You sketch, too?" said Tarragon. "Oh, you must draw Miss L'Hommedieu, she'd love that." She began gathering up the detritus of their lunch. "Will you sketch her tonight?"

"I can try," he said, and was relieved to be finished with his résumé of still another dysfunctional family.

"Then let's go back and tell her. *That*," said Tarragon," will be *much* more fun than checkers or Parcheesi."

Dinner was tomato soup enhanced by herbs, accompanied by thick slices of Gussie's homemade bread. And Leo had an announcement to make.

"I've been reading Horace again this afternoon," he said. "Very wise philosopher, and I would like to quote a few chosen lines from his work that ought to interest Andrew. Or *benefit* him," he added.

Andrew thought his manner rather sly, even mischievous, and presently understood that Leo was again proselytizing.

Clearing his throat, his soup cooling, Leo read in a dramatic voice:

> " *'True riches mean not revenues;*
>   *Care clings to wealth; the thirst for more*
>   *Grows as our fortunes grow. I stretch my store by*
>   *narrowing my wants.'* "

Here he paused to give Andrew a pointed glance before resuming:

" 'We are not poor
   While naught we seek. Happiest to whom high heaven
   Enough—no more—with sparing hand has given.' "

Andrew was impressed but nevertheless thought that heaven's hand had been rather too sparing with its gifts for the occupants of Thale's Folly—or squatters as his father would no doubt call them. "Very good, Leo," he said with a grin. "And by coincidence my father's name is Horace, too, although not as wise as your Greek friend."

"And your soup is getting cold," Gussie told him.

Leo only said, "Hmph!," lowered his head, and returned to his dinner.

Andrew's pledge to sketch Miss L'Hommedieu that evening had not only caused much interest but needed considerable organizing, since he had no materials except a pen and pencil, and preferring chiaroscuro he asked if there might be any charcoal in the house. Leo believed there was still some in the basement, and following this there was need of a blank sheet of paper and something to lean it against. In the end the blank side of a roll of wallpaper was secured to a sheet of cardboard, and the cardboard propped against the back of a chair.

"What's chiaroscuro?" asked Tarragon.

They had all moved their chairs close to watch, and he felt rather like a harpist about to play after-dinner music for them. "It's this," he said, and with the flat of the charcoal he grayed the white paper. "It's not line drawing, it's using light and shade to bring a face *out* of a background."

It felt a long time since he'd sketched. With an eraser he

picked out the highlights of cheekbones and jaw, and after studying Miss L'Hommedieu's face for a moment he began to draw: the almost skeletal figure draped in chiffon scarves, the layers of satin turban on the head shading the face but not entirely the eyes, which were black as opals . . . the imperial nose, the thin stern lips . . .

Tarragon, leaning closer, said excitedly, "She's actually coming out of the paper—it's Miss L'Hommedieu!"

"Is it flattering?" inquired Miss L'Hommedieu.

"Of course," Andrew told her.

She nodded. "I was known once for my charm. I listened to people, refusing all conversation about myself; I queried, asked, responded, and was praised for my intelligence and my wit."

"All by saying nothing?" said Andrew in surprise.

"That is the art of charm, isn't it?" she asked with a shrug. "Besides, I had no conversation."

"You were mysterious, then," said Andrew.

She smiled upon him fondly. "You see that, yes."

"It sounds rather Victorian," he told her. "People talk now, but nobody listens."

"We believe," said Gussie, "that Miss L'Hommedieu in a past life was Isadora Duncan."

"Who was strangled by her scarf," Andrew pointed out.

Gussie regarded him reproachfully. "Everyone dies *somehow*, Mr. Thale, or they wouldn't be alive today."

This gave Andrew pause. "Are you referring to theosophy? . . . don't turn your head, Miss L'Hommedieu . . . do you mean you're all reincarnated or something like that?"

Gussie smiled. "You don't feel it?"

"I don't feel much of anything these days," he told her.

Miss L'Hommedieu said sternly, "I insisted—wanting your character explained—that Tarragon tell me what work you really do. She said you write books."

"Used to."

"What kind?" asked Leo.

"Mystery novels." Glancing at Miss L'Hommedieu, he said, "You must know how satisfying it is to write a story." He added quickly, "Even if you don't write middles."

"Or endings," put in Tarragon.

Leo said, "Murder mysteries? *Real* murders?"

Andrew added a shadow to Miss L'Hommedieu's turban, saying, "No, I wrote sophisticated, made-up murders."

He received an ironic glance from Miss L'Hommedieu. "And have you ever met a murderer, even a sophisticated one?"

"I'm only twenty-six," he told her. "No."

"Murder is *not* sophisticated," she said tartly. "It's about secrets."

"Yes," he agreed, "but the fun of it is unmasking those secrets, the working out of the puzzle on paper that was fascinating. The mechanics of it, building the characters, making them real and the motives plausible and the murderer the person least suspected."

But Miss L'Hommedieu appeared to have lost interest. "Really?" she said, and rose from her chair. She added with dignity, "Whatever happened to frustrate your writing of books, Andrew, it will pass. And then it will be wise to remem-

ber that Shakespeare said, 'Let us not burden our remem-
brances with a heaviness that's gone.' "

With this she swept out of the room in a cloud of chiffon,
leaving the drawing incomplete and Andrew furious at her
certainty that his malaise would pass. How carelessly she dismissed his nightmares, he thought crossly, and then saw Tarragon watching him and smiled. He realized that he would
always smile at Tarragon, and he wondered if he was falling in
love with her, with her gift of enchantment, her sureness, and
her almost celestial loveliness. At fifty, he thought, she would
still be beautiful, and he put aside the charcoal, unpinned
Miss L'Hommedieu's portrait from the board and said that
yes, he would play a game of checkers before retiring for the
night.

Tuesday

5

Mercury claims the Dominion over [Summer Savory]. . . .
Keep it dry by you all the yeer if you love your selves and
your ease, as 'tis an hundred pound to a penny if you do not.
  —Nicholas Culpeper, *The Complete Herball*, 1652

Andrew had never slept so well. He wondered, on waking, if Manuel had found a tire for the Mercedes yet, and he hoped not. He wondered, too, if he would feel compelled to return the car to New York whether he wanted to or not, a matter of submission versus assertion. Buttoning his last clean shirt, he could hear Leo and Tarragon talking down the hall. Rather than interrupt what sounded a very serious discussion he headed for the stairs and, descending, heard the murmur of voices from the kitchen. Gussie had company.

He was halfway down the stairs when he tripped and swore out loud at his clumsiness; the voices abruptly stopped, the screen door slammed, and when he walked into the kitchen he saw through the window a woman hurrying toward the path that led to the pond. She wore baggy, paint-stained jeans, and there seemed to him something familiar about her long stride.

"Who was that?" he asked, watching her disappear among the tall grasses.

"Neighbor," Gussie said, busy scrubbing a dish at the sink. "Lives across the pond in the Bide-A-Wee cottage."

He shrugged. "Something familiar about her, I don't know what."

"Or why," said Gussie tartly, "since you saw her only from the rear. She brought us a jar of homemade orange marmalade you can spread on your toast." Fussing over a tentlike wire contraption on the kerosene stove, she produced a slice of toast, leaned over the second burner, removed a pot of boiling water, poured it into a teapot, and brought him his breakfast tea.

"What sort of tea this morning?" he asked with interest.

"Chamomile—tonic for nerves and appetite. Very calming."

He nodded. "Thank you." And with a sigh, "I suppose I'd better go and see Manuel this morning about the car."

Gussie gave him an amused glance, but said only, "Today's the day Leo's pension check should be coming if the government's behaving itself. If you wait for Artemus's mail delivery he'll give you a ride to the highway."

But Andrew's thoughts had strayed elsewhere, and he asked curiously, "How much would it cost to have your electricity connected again? I mean, so you could have tub baths and flush the toilet and board up the outhouse."

"Hah," she sniffed, "I can tell you *that* in round numbers. We owe one hundred twenty-one dollars and sixty-three cents in arrears, and heaven only knows—a small fortune—to connect us again." She gave him a sharp glance. "We manage very well, thank you, if that's what you're thinking. Of course for Miss L'Hommedieu—well, it's hardest for her, I admit."

"Are you—or were you, by any chance—a nurse?" he asked.

She vigorously shook her head. "Miss Thale's companion and housekeeper I was." She smiled, her plain face suddenly radiant. "And a rare woman she was, Miss Thale. Spunky. A rebel, you might say, and kinder than anyone *I* ever knew."

Andrew grinned. "Yes, I've met Mr. Branowski . . . I hear the gypsies arrive next?"

"Oh, she was always glad to see *them*," said Gussie, positively glowing now. "Spoke their language, you know. They called her Drabarni, the herb woman—she always had herbs waiting to give them."

"You can't mean she spoke their *actual* language," he said.

Gussie smiled. "Truth is—you might as well know, being her great-nephew—she ran away with the gypsies when she was fifteen. Lived with them a year in spite of her parents sending the police after her." She laughed. "And from what I hear she gave those police a run for their money, and some very fresh talk when they found her! Called them *sleevers*, that was the word she used. Good-for-nothings."

He said in astonishment, "You're speaking of *my great-aunt Harriet Thale*?"

She gave him a knowing look. "Be a good thing for you if *you* had a few of her genes. She used to quote some Greek man who said everybody needed a dose of wildness to set them free."

Set them free . . . *he* didn't feel free. He thought gloomily,

"And all I've accomplished at twenty-six is a nervous break-down."

He wasn't aware that he'd spoken his thought aloud until Gussie turned and said to him in a matter-of-fact voice, "Oh, she had one of those, too. They shut her up when they got her back, her parents. Not that she was mad, but in those days a girl like Harriet Thale was bred to be a debutante and marry well, and of course she was a terrible embarrassment."

Just what his father had said of her, he remembered, and suddenly laughed. "Well, well!" he said, and wondered if his father had ever experienced a single moment of wildness.

And if I ever could, he thought somberly, and considering this he realized how bloodless the characters in his two mystery novels seemed to him just now.

Seeing the look on his face, Gussie said sternly, "You can never tell about people. They wear masks, you know, they're like icebergs showing only what they please, and they die full of secrets. You'll be blessed, Andrew, if you come to know—really know—just a handful of people in a lifetime."

Startled, he said, "Do you feel you came to really know my great-aunt?"

She nodded. "I had that honor, yes." She smiled. "Except I never did learn—or ask, either—what she would never tell her parents."

"And what was that?"

Gussie chuckled. "Whether she was still a virgin when the police found her." She stopped, her head tilted, listening. "I hear a car. Artemus is early, that's his mail jeep."

Leo came hurrying down the stairs. "Mail delivery!" he shouted, and shot out of the door like a bolt of lightning.

"Well now," Gussie said, wiping her hands on her apron and looking pleased. She, too, walked out to welcome Artemus, and Andrew, still in a state of amazement, followed her.

"Just the person I want to see," Artemus told Andrew. "Leo, here's your government check right on time, you don't need to plot the overthrow of the government *this* month." Giving Andrew a sober look, "I've got a message for you from Manuel. He tells me there's a man been keeping his eye on your car in the garage, and as sheriff here I've got to ask what the hell's going on. Manuel says he drove up the highway last evening after dinner to visit his mother, and he was followed all the way to Pittsville. Seems the man thought Manuel would lead him to *you*. Same man, a black Chevy. Manuel says you better not show yourself at the garage this morning. Care to explain?"

Baffled, Andrew shook his head. "I can't. It's hard to believe this myself, there has to be a mistake somewhere."

Artemus's eyes narrowed. "Manuel's very definite about it being the *owner* of the Mercedes this man is looking for."

Andrew brightened. "Well, there's the mistake, you see, I'm not the owner. It's a company car, Meredith Machines, Incorporated."

Artemus said dryly, "You may have to explain that to the man yourself." With a glance at his watch he started up the engine of his jeep. "Already half-past eight. Left my wife in charge of the post office, got to get back now but Manuel was afraid you might walk in to see him this morning. Said to tell you the tire's to be delivered late afternoon today or first thing tomorrow, he'll send his son Manuel Junior to tell you when."

He turned the jeep smartly around in the driveway and began weaving his way past potholes until he disappeared around the curve in the road.

Returning to the house, Andrew collected notebook and camera and mounted the stairs to dutifully record and count bedrooms for his father. He hoped he wasn't about to add a new torment to his lost writing career, that of his great-aunt Harriet, whose genes he had apparently not inherited, since he would no doubt compliantly drive the restored car back to Manhattan, as instructed, and probably continue the only writing of which he was capable now: *Margo Johnson in Receiving is recently returned from a two-week vacation in Ireland, where she paid a visit to our nuts-and-bolts factory outside of Dublin . . . Jim Morton in Design is the happy father of a new son, Jason . . . Our merger is proceeding with great success, and it promises . . .* "Promises four thousand workers fired," he said aloud, angrily.

Beginning his research he opened the door to a closet and then to a bathroom, where he stood amazed at a bathtub so huge and antique that it was set in a magnificent base of mahogany, its interior lined with tin. This was a surprise, and he made a note of it.

Of bedrooms he counted six, and with each door left open, he was allowed to view them without guilt, identifying the occupant of each by its furnishings. Leo's room startled him: it was so filled with books it was difficult to locate his bed;

books on long shelves reaching to the ceiling, in piles on the floor and stacked high on the table next to his narrow bed.

Tarragon's room he found intriguing and rather touching: on her walls she had taped exotic pictures cut from *National Geographics*: a sunset over the Indian Ocean; a man—Burmese or Chinese—tilling the soil; a smiling young woman in a sarong; a view of lateens with richly colored sails against a purple sea—black faces, brown faces, white faces, sunsets and sunrises, and he wondered if this was *her* dream.

At the far end of the hall, removed from the others, he knew at once whose room it was because of the table under the window, on which stood an arrangement similar to what he'd seen in the woods: two candles, an incense burner, and a plate heaped with wildflowers. Altar or shrine, this belonged to the resident witch, of course. Remembering that Tarragon had described incantations as prayers he wondered, if this was true, what prayers had been said, and to whom, in this austere and sunny room. Not many could have been answered, he thought, considering their situation here, and if she had prayed they might remain in this house, his arrival had put an end to that.

Staring at the simple offerings on the table he realized all the consequences of his visit.

And yet—if he'd not come?

He could protest, argue and plead, but his father had never been accessible to pleas. His father moved in a straight and undeviating line.

Turning away he walked back down the hall to the fifth

bedroom, which was the room he occupied, made a note of it, and turned to the open door across the hall. Stepping inside he found Miss L'Hommedieu seated by the window, her back to him. Apparently she had not heard him, and he glanced around him with curiosity. The room was quite bare except for a large mirror over a bureau on which stood a glass jar holding an eruption of peacock feathers; a small trunk under the window, a neatly made bed with a trail of chiffon tossed across it. And Miss L'Hommedieu.

She turned her head. "Good morning, Andrew," she said courteously. "You are counting the rooms, I see."

"How did you know?"

"I am not deaf. I was just listening to a wood thrush in the tree outside, it sings a beautiful song." She looked him over with her penetrating, ironic gaze and said, "Well, Andrew?"

Startled, he said, "Well *what*?"

"Gussie's magic brought you here, what do you plan to do about it?"

He looked at her with exasperation. "What do you mean, Gussie's magic brought me here?"

"We needed help."

"I can't help anybody, not even myself," he told her. "As for magic, forget it. My father sent me here and I can assure you that nobody waved a wand over him."

"You're a very narrow-minded young man. Promising, yes, but narrow. Magic," she said simply, "is actually God's grace."

"Well, He didn't send me either. Isn't anyone acquainted with reality here?"

"We're speaking of reality, are we?" she inquired with the lift of an eyebrow.

"Yes. Reality is twenty-five acres and a house that was never deeded to—"

She held up a hand. "Enough!"

"Enough what?"

"Of reality. Once—long ago—I met with Reality," she said, "and found it so pitiless and chilling that I have taken great care to avoid it ever since. You may go now, Andrew, I prefer my wood thrush."

Feeling dismissed, and aware that he'd been cross and even rude, he went downstairs, thoroughly chastised. Gussie was in the kitchen peeling potatoes, the door and windows open to the warm and hazy morning and to the shrilling of locusts in the woods. He said, "Where's Tarragon?"

"Thinning the kale in the garden."

He watched Gussie for a moment and then said, "There must be something I can do. To help."

She gave him an appraising glance. "Pick blueberries?"

"Right. Where do I find them?"

She opened a cupboard door and brought out two bowls. "There's a field over near Bald Hill, not far," she told him. "You cross where Wally Blore was digging and take the path to the right."

With a glance through the window Andrew said, "He's not there."

"Paid and gone," said Gussie cryptically, and he thought her glance at him held mockery.

With a nod he carried away the bowls, shouted a hello to

Tarragon, seated in the long row of kale, and set out in the direction of Bald Hill.

Ten minutes later he emerged from the woods into a meadow where trees had given way to tangles of grass, thistles, burdock, and scrub. *Wild blueberries, not packaged in plastic,* he reminded himself, and obviously hidden by overgrowth and needing a keen eye to find. He stepped carefully through the tall grass, peering down and into it for a glimpse of blue concealed among the shadows. There was dew still on the grass and a faint movement of air, not yet a breeze; the grass resisted his passage, and he began stamping it down to create a path. *At least I'm creating something, if only a path,* he thought, *why must there always be this hunger to create with words?* Leaning over to inspect what lay in the shadows of a tall bush he found a site rich with blue and sat down, heedless of damp grass. Stretching out a hand he began to cull the berries from their stems, dropping them into a bowl.

The sun was warm, and the unbroken silence was no longer menacing to him now but soothing. Seated here on the ground, half concealed among the tall grasses, he felt a very real pleasure in this connection with the earth, and crammed a handful of berries into his mouth. They tasted of fresh air, cool and moist and delicious.

A bush nearby gently stirred; a bird had arrived on a branch to watch him, a bright yellow bird with black wings, and Andrew bid him good morning. At the sound of his voice the branch swayed wildly but the yellow bird refused flight and gave a small chirp of acknowledgment.

It marked Andrew, this moment.

He found himself thinking, *What a wonderful place this would be for writing—if only I could write.*

But he had nothing to write of, nothing that interested or excited him, and he carefully put that thought aside and returned to picking blueberries.

When he retraced his steps, after an hour in the sun, he found that he had left paths of flattened grass all through the field behind him, and his two bowls were heaped with berries, still with a faint sheen from the morning dew.

Gussie was no longer in the kitchen. He left the two bowls on the table and walked out onto the porch just as Manuel's pickup truck pulled into the drive and came to a noisy stop. He expected to see Manuel, but when the door opened it was his father who stepped out, looking totally out of place in his impeccable linen jacket, well-cut slacks and polished loafers.

"Good God," Andrew said incredulously. "*You?*"

It was a shock, this collision of two worlds.

His father glared at him, both hands on his hips. He said furiously, "My car is being towed out of a ditch near the post office, and that insufferable man at the garage refused to drive me here himself in this—this *truck*—with the excuse that he might be followed here and put you in danger. I cannot *conceive* of what is going on here, or—" He stopped, his gaze widening to include the house. "Selkirk said this wreck is *occupied?*"

"*Not* a wreck," said Andrew defiantly. "Still a very comfortable old-fashioned farmhouse—lacking a few amenities, it's true—but four people manage to live here very well."

"You've known this since Saturday, Andrew? You found *squatters* here and didn't call the police?"

His father had called them squatters, just as he'd expected. "You'll have to call the police yourself, Father."

"Then lead me to the phone."

"There isn't one. And the people living here were all friends of your aunt Harriet Thale, Father. Surely you can't turn them out!"

"My dear Andrew, Harriet Thale has been dead for five years, of course I can turn them out. I've come here, not only to take you back to New York, but to tell you flatly that you're no longer needed here because—"

Andrew heard himself say—much to his surprise—"But I *am* needed, I've just been told this morning that I'm needed."

"—because yesterday," continued his father, "I contacted by phone a realtor in this neighborhood and found him extremely interested in bidding on these twenty-five acres. He mentioned a very substantial sum, I might add. We had a long talk on the phone. He said he could envision twenty or twenty-five Swiss chalets for summer people, a swimming pool, and a fitness room, all very salable."

"Swiss chalets?" said Andrew incredulously. "Twenty-five of them, and a fitness room? You'd turn them out for that? You'd be that cruel?"

"In business," said his father, "the word is *detached*. Such an offer would be one I could scarcely refuse—"

"—as if you haven't enough money," Andrew said hotly.

His father smiled. "It's money that sent you to private

schools, Andrew, and gave you every advantage. Your anger is entirely inappropriate, you've allowed sentiment to overtake you, and in business there is no place at all for sentiment."

"Like firing four thousand people at Meredith Machines?"

His father sighed. "You can scarcely equate removing four squatters, illegally occupying my property, with the streamlining of a corporation."

"It shows the same indifference—or *detachment*," he flung at him.

"That's *your* viewpoint, Andrew. Now get your clothes, or whatever you brought with you, and let's return to New York where you belong. You've already missed two days of work, and it has embarrassed me no end, covering for you."

"The Mercedes isn't repaired yet."

"It will be sent for later."

"I'm not going, Father."

He said warningly, "I can't hold your job for you indefinitely, Andrew. You can't possibly be serious."

"Completely serious, Father. Besides," Andrew said firmly, "after Mr. Branowski, we can expect the gypsies."

His father stared at him blankly. "I have no idea what you're talking about, Andrew."

"I know that . . . Have a good trip back, Father." He turned on his heel and was horrified to see that Gussie had been standing on the porch, where she must have overheard every word of their angry exchange. She looked stricken, and disappeared quickly into the house while his father, furious, climbed back into the pickup truck, fumbled with the gears and reversed the truck at an insane speed, then turned and drove down the road and out of sight.

"And may you end up in a pothole for shouting about Swiss chalets," Andrew said bitterly, but nevertheless felt a little sick from the confrontation.

He also felt depressed, an effect his father had on him these days whenever they met.

Footsteps on the gravel overtook him, and a hand was slipped into his: it was Tarragon.

"Has Gussie told them?" he asked.

"Only me."

"Will Gussie cry?"

"Gussie never cries. She'll finish making potato soup for our lunch and then, unless it rains," she added with a glance at the graying sky, "she'll take her robe and incense burner into the woods to her shrine. Maybe even if it rains."

"And do what?" he asked cynically.

"Why, she'll call on the powers of the Mother Goddess and Father God—and on the Earth, Air, Fire, and Water, Sun, Moon, and Stars . . . it sounds lovely, doesn't it?" she said. "We live so close to them all, they must surely hear her."

He had to admit the poetic cadence of the powers to whom Gussie would appeal, but he remained skeptical. "You've seen her do this?"

"Oh no—never," Tarragon said. "That's private and sacred, but when Mr. Branowski was so very sick she did light blue candles in the room—blue for healing—and I'd hear her speaking words over him, and she went often into the woods.

And he recovered." She added gravely, "Gussie said you were very brave with your father, I saw him from the window. He looked—" She hesitated.

"Looked what?" he asked.

"Like a man who grinds his teeth all the time."

Andrew smiled. "I'm sure of *that*." His smile quickly faded as he thought of the disaster his father's teeth-grinding could wreak upon Gussie, Miss L'Hommedieu, and Leo. He said soberly, "We should find something to cheer her up, or at least distract her, until the shock passes. Leo got his pension check this morning, where does he cash it?"

"Artemus cashes it for him, and then Leo and I catch the bus out on the highway into Pittsville and buy the groceries we can carry. The kerosene and powdered milk—heavy things—we buy from Artemus. And sometimes, when there's leftover money, we go to the thrift shop."

He frowned. "Let me go with you tomorrow . . . There should be *something*—let me think about it." But he didn't know what could possibly distract them from the prospect of losing their home.

He did not have long to think. They had just finished lunch when the sound of a car was heard in the driveway.

"Never had so much traffic before," grumbled Leo. "Beats all. Third car today!" He rose to peer out the window.

Andrew was even more curious as to who had managed to escape the potholes; he rose, too. One glance and he said, "Good God!"

"What is it?" asked Gussie.

"It's the Mercedes, the car that Manuel's been repairing,

but why on earth—returning it *here* is what he said he'd never do."

They hurried out onto the porch as a small boy climbed out of the car, looking no more than ten years old, his freckled face shaded by a Boston Red Sox baseball cap.

"You drove that?" Andrew gasped in dismay. "At your age, and without a driver's license?"

"Garn," the child said, "only drove a mile down the highway, nobody'd see me. And I know all the holes in Thale's Road." To Andrew he said, "I'm Manuel Junior, my dad was too busy to come himself. He said to wish you a safe trip back to New York now the car's fixed, and here's the bill. And since you're leaving now there's no need to worry 'bout that stranger who's been hanging around."

"Except that I'm *not* leaving," protested Andrew.

Manuel Junior looked at him blankly. "But your car's *fixed* now."

"Yes, but didn't Mr. Thale—my father—tell Manuel I'm not returning to New York yet, that I'm—" He stopped, because of course his father would have left in a fury, too angry to do more than pay his bill and drive away.

"Did anyone follow you?" asked Tarragon.

"Ho!" said young Manuel. "On that road?"

"Ho yourself," said Andrew, and shrugged; after all, the horse was out of the barn, and the milk spilled, so to speak. He brought out his checkbook and paid the boy.

 Manuel Junior left, to walk home by the shortcut. Tarragon, Miss L'Hommedieu, and Gussie returned to the house, but Andrew stood looking at the car, so unexpectedly delivered, sleek and shining, a car that purred. His father had recklessly said that it would be sent for, and it could jolly well be sent for, decided Andrew. In the meantime, there it stood.

Andrew said to Leo, "We could drive this car to Pittsville this afternoon, and you could all go . . . all of you. No bus."

"In a Mercedes?" said Leo, eyeing it suspiciously. "And me a union man. Belong to you?"

"No, it's a company car."

"Strictly for the bigwigs, eh?"

"Yes. We'd borrow it."

Leo glanced at him with interest. "Borrow it?"

"I suspect," said Andrew with dignity, "that by now I, too, have been downsized. It wants revenge."

Leo nodded approvingly. "Brings out the larceny in a man, don't it? By George, you'll be a revolutionary yet, Andrew!"

6

[Marigold] must be taken only when the moon is in the Sign
of the Virgin . . . And the gatherer, who must be out of
deadly sin, must say three Pater Nosters and three Aves. It
will give the wearer a vision of anyone who has robbed him.
—Macer, Floridus, *Herbal*, 1373

On the second floor of the house there was suddenly a
flurry of activity. Leo could be heard swearing at the
disappearance of a bow tie; Miss L'Hommedieu had already
been escorted downstairs in rusty black, enlivened by a long
pink chiffon scarf that fluttered behind her. Andrew, review-
ing his several travel checks, shoved them into the pocket of
his tweed jacket along with his wallet, and extracted his raincoat from the closet. The act of tossing it over his arm produced a jingling sound; one hand delved into the left pocket
and brought out a pair of keys on a thin silver ring.

Andrew looked at them blankly, but—*time later,* he thought,
*to puzzle out whether they were spare keys to office or apart-
ment, and why they were there at all;* he dropped these into
the pocket of his jacket, too, and carrying his raincoat

emerged from his room just as Gussie came hurrying down the hall.

"Oh, but you won't need your raincoat," she told him. "Just look outside, sky's clearing!"

"Good," said Andrew, relieved, and went back and tossed the raincoat across his bed and followed her down the stairs.

What a motley group, he thought, seeing them waiting beside the car: Gussie, plain and practical in a flowered housedress; Miss L'Hommedieu towering above her, thin, shabby but somehow elegant; Leo, short, stocky, and bow-tied; and Tarragon in a short white skirt and T-shirt, her eyes shining.

"Well, Andrew?" said Miss L'Hommedieu, allowing him to bestow her in a rear seat. "You must be very rich, a car like this!"

"Not mine," said Andrew cheerfully. "And somehow we've got to avoid the potholes, we can't risk another three days in a garage. Tarragon?"

"I know them," she said, and took command of the passenger seat, leaning forward in anticipation, ready to point and to direct.

Slowly, carefully, the car made its way successfully to the highway, turned left, away from Manuel's garage and the post office, and headed for Pittsville.

The grocery store was obviously a treat: Andrew led Miss L'Hommedieu up and down the aisles while Gussie, Leo, and Tarragon fanned out to look for yeast and flour, honey, eggs, and boxes of dried milk, but the thrift shop proved to be the high point of the trip. Andrew had expected the worst, a covey of unwashed Mr. Branowskis, perhaps, a certain dis-reputable ambience . . . He was to be surprised: it occupied a well-lit room, quite large, with long racks of clothes, and an alcove of old books toward which Leo went at once. There was a chair on which Miss L'Hommedieu could sit, and in the rear a number of baby carriages, lamps, and radios.

A prominently displayed sign read: IF YOU STEAL FROM US, YOU ARE STEALING FROM HOMELESS WOMEN AND CHILDREN.

Very good, thought Andrew, and after glancing at a shabby, but still-fine tweed jacket with a price tag of thirteen dollars, he experienced the inevitable excitement of capturing a bargain, accompanied by an expanding sense of greed.

In the end, however, he bought nothing for himself be-cause his eyes had fallen on a long feathered boa in Miss L'Hommedieu's favorite color of pale blue. He touched it, and its feathers stirred under his touch; he looked at the price tag—ten dollars—and he envisioned her sweeping it dramati-cally across one shoulder. He turned and looked at her, seated primly in her chair, very erect, a little tired, her face composed as she waited for them, and he plucked it from the hanger and carried it to her.

"If you will allow me, Miss L'Hommedieu," he said politely, and with a flourish he unfurled it around her shoulders. "You simply must—it's *you*—unless, of course—"

"Unless?"

"Unless you don't like it. If you do, it's yours, I insist."

A wave of pink flooded her cheeks: Miss L'Hommedieu was blushing. She also looked extraordinarily pleased—surely she'd been given gifts before? "This is most gracious of you, Andrew," she said, and reached out and stroked the feathers, watching them stir. "It's beautiful—thank you!"

"Good, it's yours," he told her, and carried it off to pay for it.

After that he ran wild. "Everything's my treat," he told them, and insisted that Tarragon try on a black jacket glittering with sequins. "But I'll never wear it," she told him, laughing. "Andrew, truly you've gone mad."

"I have, yes," he said, grinning. "Time to sober up later, it fits and you look dazzling in it."

When they returned to the car each of them bore treasures: Gussie, a warm cardigan, a new apron, and two old cookbooks; Leo, paperback copies of *Moby-Dick*, Montaigne's *Essays, Don Quixote*, and Plato's *Republic*; Tarragon, the glittering sequin jacket and half a dozen *National Geographics*. As for Miss L'Hommedieu she eagerly clutched her long, feathered blue boa, alternately hugging and stroking it.

For at least an hour or two, thought Andrew, he had given them an antidote for the shock that lay ahead. And for only forty-six dollars and twenty-three cents.

Possibly, he added ruefully, he had also assuaged some of his guilts at *possessing* forty-six dollars and twenty-three cents.

On the way back to Thale's Folly, and after considerable thought, Andrew stopped at the post office; dropping coins into the pay phone he left word with his father's answering service that after ten o'clock the next morning a repaired Mercedes would be at Manuel's garage for someone to pick up and return to Manhattan. He felt only a small twinge of conscience;

it was true that it was he who had driven the car to Thale's Folly, but the expedition and the Mercedes had been entirely his father's idea, and Andrew was still unforgiving.

After this, with Tarragon's help, he again began the slow and precarious drive up Thale Road to the house.

It was Miss L'Hommedieu who first noticed that something was wrong. From the rear seat, leaning forward, she said indignantly, "My chair's been moved."

This was true. Her chair had sat like a throne in a commanding position on the porch but it had now been thrust to one side.

Andrew brought the car to a stop and Tarragon, climbing out, shaded her eyes against the late afternoon sun and said, "The back door's open, Gussie."

"Nonsense, I locked it," Gussie told her.

"It's open, Gussie, just look. *Wide* open."

Andrew looked at Leo, and Leo looked at him. "Help Miss L'Hommedieu out," he told Tarragon, "we're going in."

"I insist," said Miss L'Hommedieu firmly, "that you wait for me."

They waited, and all five entered the house together.

Nothing had been touched in the kitchen, no one had been interested in the glass jars of herbs or the preserves lined up in the pantry, nor had anything been moved or removed in the living room, dining room, or parlor; they together mounted the stairs, slowing only to help Miss L'Hommedieu.

It was Andrew's room that appeared to have been swept by a tornado. They stood in the doorway staring aghast at the chaos:

the mirror that had once hung over the bureau had been hurled to the floor, its brown paper backing slashed and torn away, leaving paper strewn everywhere. Fragments of glass lay scattered across the floor, and Andrew's bed had been stripped, its mattress slit open, rolled up and reduced to a mass of coils and stuffing. His raincoat lay in shreds on the floor.

"I don't understand this," faltered Gussie.

"Rage—act of a madman!" said Leo.

"But why?" demanded Andrew.

"We need a broom," announced Miss L'Hommedieu.

Andrew stepped carefully over the glass to the mirror and picked it up, fragments of glass dropping from it like slivers of silver rain. "Tarragon, watch out for this glass," he said.

"Fetch the broom, Leo," Gussie told him. "Miss L'Hommedieu, don't come inside, stay in the hall."

"I am not breakable," said Miss L'Hommedieu calmly. "We must remain calm, very calm."

Tarragon advanced into the room, picked up the remains of Andrew's raincoat, shook it free of glass, and tossed it onto the skeletal frame of the bed. One sleeve, intact, fell to the floor. Picking it up she looked at it and frowned. "Andrew, there's something funny about this."

"Funny! It's a disaster!"

"I mean the sleeve. Andrew, look at this sleeve."

"Later." He was returning the frame of the mirror to the bureau.

"Andrew, look at it. *Please.*"

She held up the sleeve, and he glanced at it. "I'm looking . . . so?"

"It's too big. It's much longer than your arm, it belongs to a *giant*."

Leo, returning, said, "I've got the broom. What's going on?"

Tarragon had picked up the remains of the coat and was examining its collar. "Very well, then, Andrew," she said sternly, "what size coat or jacket do you wear?"

He decided that obviously, in a crisis, she had to find security in details; he would have to remember this in the future. "Forty long," he said.

"The label on this raincoat says it's forty-eight regular."

She had captured his attention at last. "Impossible, let me look at it—what's left of it."

She stepped over the broken glass and pressed the sleeve against Andrew's shoulder. "Drop your arm."

He obeyed; the sleeve ran from his shoulder to his wrist and dangled several inches beyond it. He said in a shocked voice, "This isn't my coat! Is there a label?"

"Here," she told him. "It says Christian Dior."

"I've never worn a Christian Dior in my life!" He stared at it, dumbfounded. "But where—oh God," he said as memory surfaced to surprise him. "The *restaurant*!"

"What restaurant?" asked Gussie.

"On my way here from New York. The coats hung on pegs in the hall. I drove away without mine—forgot it—and then drove back, rushed into the restaurant, and picked up my coat and—"

He stopped.

"And?"

He looked stricken. "As I drove away a man ran out of the

restaurant waving frantically. I saw him in my rearview mirror and assumed he thought I'd left without paying my bill." He sat down suddenly on the rolled-up mattress. "Good Lord, he wanted my raincoat? I mean *his* raincoat?"

Miss L'Hommedieu said disapprovingly, "And for this he broke into the house and ruined Andrew's and Miss Thale's bed and mirror? The world has come to *this*?"

Frowning, Tarragon said, "He knew we'd all left the house and it was empty, but how?"

"Manuel Junior," said Andrew grimly. *"Of course* Manuel Junior. Our burglar must have been the man that Manuel told me kept hanging around his garage, asking who belonged to the Mercedes, and when Manuel made the mistake of delivering the car *here*, the man followed it."

"Then why the hell didn't he take his damned raincoat?" demanded Leo. "Look at it—he found it, sliced it up and left it. Doesn't make a particle of sense."

Andrew whistled softly through his teeth. "Unless . . . unless . . ." He reached into the pocket of his jacket and extracted the two keys on their ring. "Could he have been after these?"

Startled, Tarragon said, "Where did you find *those*?"

"In the pocket of my raincoat—I mean *his* raincoat. Just before we left for town. I thought it was going to rain, I picked up the coat to carry on my arm, heard them jingle, so I took them out and shoved them into the pocket of *this* jacket. I assumed they were mine. After all, it was my coat, or so I thought. And then—you remember, Gussie—you said I wouldn't need a raincoat so I put it back. But not the keys."

"Artemus," said Leo.

Gussie nodded. "Definitely Artemus."

"Artemus?" said Andrew blankly.

"He's the sheriff here."

"He did mention that, yes." Andrew sighed. "It's nearly dark, I don't dare drive the Mercedes again, it's not mine."

"I'll go," Tarragon said. "By the shortcut, walking. The post office is closed, he'll be at his house. Save my dinner, I'll run." And she was gone before Andrew could volunteer either his company or his flashlight.

"I suppose we should save the evidence for him?" he said doubtfully. "It's not the same as a murder scene, not exactly, but will he want to see the room as we found it?"

"Not if he cuts a foot on the glass and gets blood poisoning," Gussie said tartly. "Leo, after you've swept up the glass fetch the spare mattress in the attic for Andrew." With a nod at the yellowed papers strewn among the splinters of glass she added, "And don't throw *them* away. Good for kindling and the mulch pile. I'll heat up dinner."

Artemus arrived in Manuel's tow truck, red and blue lights flashing, a spotlight trained on the hazardous pitfalls of Thale's Road. Manuel was driving. "Because," explained Tarragon as the two men vanished upstairs, "Manuel can describe the man who was so interested in finding you."

Artemus was not long upstairs. "Snapped a few photos," he said, "and I'll take those keys with me, Andrew, and give you a receipt for them. Lock them up in my safe."

"Any clues?" asked Andrew, feeling absurdly like a character in one of his novels. "You think that's what he was after?"

"He certainly wasn't after his raincoat," said Artemus. "Good night, Gussie . . . Tarragon . . . Leo . . . Miss L'Hommedieu."

It had been a busy day. There had been no story from Miss L'Hommedieu, the sunset had not been observed, nor had Gussie had time to visit the woods to call on the powers of earth, fire, sun, and moon. Nevertheless, various stars had begun crossing and events set in motion, unrecognized or noticed as yet. At least not until night, when a sleepless Andrew looked for reading material.

Wednesday

7

As for Rosmarine, I lett it runne all over my garden walls, not onlie because my bees love it, but because it is the herb sacred to remembrance, and, therefore, to friendship. . . .

—Sir Thomas More

It was an hour past midnight when Andrew, shouting, ran down the hall with his flashlight. Until then the night had been so quiet one could hear the frogs croaking in the marsh near the pond, and that was a far distance.

"Wake up, wake up, I've news," he shouted.

When doors were slow to open he stood in the hall waving two sheets of paper and shouted, " 'I, Harriet Maria Thale, being of sound mind and body, and cognizant of the fact that a handwritten will is acceptable, legal, and binding in this state, do hereby—' "

Doors flew open, and Andrew stopped, triumphant.

Leo gasped, "You found a *will?*"

Andrew beamed at him. "I found a will."

Tarragon cried, "Miss Thale's will? But where, Andrew? How?"

"On the floor. In the pile set aside for mulch. Come see."

Candles were lighted and Andrew led a procession in night-gowns and pajamas back to his room. Walking over to the mirror he turned its empty face to the wall and pointed to the remaining strips of brown paper and newspapers that had lined the back of it. "I think it must have been taped or thumbtacked behind the mirror for safekeeping, and when the burglar slashed the backing—"

"The *mirror!*" said Gussie wonderingly. "We never thought of that, did we? You remember, Leo—Miss L'Hommedieu—Tarragon—we looked *everywhere!*"

"Or thought we did," said Tarragon.

Leo nodded. "She did squirrel things away, we knew that, but—"

"But what does it say?" asked Tarragon.

Gussie looked at her reproachfully. "Isn't it enough that she cared and made a will?"

Andrew gave her a sharp glance, suddenly understanding that a stoic Gussie had nursed deep hurt over Miss Thale's omission, even though she had died without any warning on a sunny day among the chives. He said gently, "It's for you to read, not me. Why don't we go down to the kitchen, light the big kerosene lamp, brew some tea, and read it?"

They did not hurry. Once in the kitchen it seemed to Andrew as if it was enough for them to know that his great-aunt Harriet had made an attempt to protect her ménage after all, and that presently they would hear her long-gone voice through the words that she had written. The kerosene lamp was carefully lighted, the wick turned up and placed in the center of the worn kitchen table, where it shone softly gold on the weathered oak. There was a silence invaded only by the murmur of water coming to boil on the stove.

Tarragon thoughtfully selected herbs from the shelf. "Rosemary and mint," she told them, smiling.

And then they sat down around the table—it was like having a family, thought Andrew, feeling warmly included—and Gussie turned to the will.

"I, Harriet Marie Thale . . ."

"When did she write it?" Leo asked gruffly.

"A year before she died, in the summer. That year we tried Jerusalem artichokes, and they rotted." Her eyes scanned the document—there was a growing suspense now—and suddenly Gussie's eyes filled with tears. "Oh, how lovely," she gasped.

"What?" asked Leo.

"She leaves the house—the house and twenty-five acres to 'my dear friend Gussie Pease.' To *me!*"

Andrew felt a disconcerting and very illicit pleasure at this. "You mean my father doesn't own Thale's Folly after all?"

A radiant Gussie was turning the page. "She writes, 'I bequeath my remaining wealth thus: To be equally divided, one half to Miss Gussie Pease, to whom I entrust the support of all occupants of Thale's Folly for so long as they live, my funds being in the form of gold, the currency of the Rom, whom I respect and hold dear (I append a separate letter explaining where this has been buried), and one half of my funds to Tarragon Sage Valerian, and *dear Tarragon, be wise about this.*' "

"There's money, too?" gasped Tarragon. "So that we can *keep* the house?"

"And the will," concluded Gussie, "has been witnessed by Abraham Branowski and Zilka Stephanovitch . . . one of Miss Thale's gypsy friends," she reminded them.

"Well!" exclaimed Andrew, happy for them. "It certainly *sounds* legal. Do you know of a good lawyer in Pittsville?"

Miss L'Hommedieu, in her long flannel nightgown, had listened intently to Gussie's reading and now, turning her penetrating black eyes on Andrew she said sternly, "Well, Andrew?"

"Well what?"

"I told you so."

Thoroughly puzzled he said, "Told me what?"

"That it would be you, after all. You have not taken thought of the sequence of events that led to this?"

They were all staring at Andrew now. He said, "I haven't the slightest idea what you mean."

"The raincoat," she said impatiently. "You don't see it? You left your raincoat in a restaurant—"

"Pure mindlessness," he put in.

"—and when you returned for it you snatched the coat of a stranger, and this madman, for reasons unknown—"

"—surely the keys," broke in Tarragon eagerly.

"This madman burglarized the house tonight, tore apart the furniture in your room, as well as the mirror, and because of this—"

"—and your mindlessness," breathed Tarragon, nodding.

"Because of this, Harriet Thale's will—behind that mirror all these years—has suddenly been found."

He supposed that it made a sort of cockeyed sense, at least to Miss L'Hommedieu. He thought that soon she would be telling him that if he'd had no nervous breakdown, had not fallen out of the sky in a plane he would never have come to Thale's Folly. And then he was stunned by the thought that no, he would *not* have driven here at his father's request, he would *not* have been writing a newsletter for Meredith Machines, and there would have been no crack-up, no writer's block, and no—oh God—no Tarragon?

At the look on his face, Miss L'Hommedieu nodded, satisfied. "Now where is the letter she left?"

Gussie turned over the two pages and frowned. "There isn't one."

They stared at her blankly. "No letter? She said a letter," pointed out Leo.

"It must be upstairs—the mulch pile," said Andrew, pushing back his chair and rising, but he was remembering that mulch pile: he had searched it for something to read—*anything*—but he could not remember a letter.

"I'll go too," said Tarragon. "You finish your tea, Gussie, you've done enough rushing about."

Upstairs, he and Tarragon approached the small pile of papers, sat down on the floor, and began sorting. "A real antique, that mirror," he said. "They padded the backs of their mirrors with anything available, and here's a scrap from a newspaper dated 1898."

"But *this* wasn't part of the backing," she said, showing him a ten-year-old tax receipt.

There were several other receipted bills, and Andrew began to have a good idea of what Gussie, Leo, and Miss L'Hommedieu had been deprived of since Miss Thale's death. There had once been electricity, hot water, a car that Manuel had serviced, books bought, a furnace that burned oil. But there was no letter.

Andrew sat back on his heels and shook his head. "No letter, Tarragon."

The glow had gone from her eyes. "Not here, Andrew, no, but surely somewhere else in the house?"

He said dryly, "Behind another mirror? But this was *her* room."

"A simple letter," she said stubbornly. "Or a map, showing where it was buried. Without it—without it we'll lose the house after all, Andrew."

"We can dig," he pointed out.

"Twenty-five acres?"

"We can dig," he said firmly.

" 'We,' Andrew?"

"Yes, we. Until the gypsies come, remember?"

"But your job!"

He ignored this and said instead, "We'd better go down and tell them that tomorrow they begin a new search of the house."

Andrew awoke at dawn exhausted and in a cold sweat. With a glance at his watch he saw that he'd slept for only three hours, and he had spent those three hours descending in slow motion to the earth, over and over, not knowing if he'd live or die; he could only hope that he'd not screamed. It was six o'clock, and outside the crickets had stilled. The house was silent; he pulled on his jeans and walked barefoot downstairs through the kitchen and out into the garden. The grass was silken and cold with dew, the sky suffused with blush pink, but although a dark closet would be kindest for him he knew a place among the cornstalks where he could hide and pull his ragged nerves together. It seemed a pity, he thought savagely, that only yesterday there had been a happy trip to a thrift shop, but it felt an aeon ago, and this morning his generosity struck him as patronizing. Darkness had settled on him, and like beads on a rosary he counted over his failures and mocked himself. A hero last evening, he thought scornfully? This had collapsed almost at once, for there was no promised letter, and being more worldly than the occupants of Thale's Folly he knew that in this case the will was meaningless without money; Gussie would at once be liable for the five years of property tax his father had paid, she would have no money for lawyers or for the estate tax, and his father could still win the house and twenty-five acres.

His great-aunt's eccentricities struck him this morning as capricious, maddening, thoughtless, and bereft of reason.

So much for *that*, but there was more, of course, because today was Wednesday, and Meredith Machines would be no more forgiving than his father, and there was no question but that he was now among the unemployed. His second and last book had been published almost two years ago, and the royalties from it were dwindling while other young authors were filling the bookstores with equally as sophisticated mystery novels, whereas he brooded here among the herbs and vegetables, his emotions and imagination bankrupt. It was doubtful that he would ever write another book. Ever.

The futility of it all, he thought bitterly.

A slight breeze stirred the cornstalks among which he had taken shelter. At the end of the row he could see Miss L'Hommedieu's chair of sturdy oak that Gussie placed there every day; on the other side of him a row of green beans marched down to a profusion of huge zucchini plants with their bugle-shaped yellow flowers. He wanted to lie down on the earth between all this growing and ripening, and lose himself in the healing earth, hiding and burying himself, too depressed to go on, unfit for human company, even Tarragon.

He lay down, pillowing his head on his arms.

A pair of pointed black shoes interrupted his black thoughts: old shoes, worn. He looked up to find Miss L'Hommedieu standing over him.

"Well, Andrew?" she said.

He sat up. "Well, *what?*" he asked crossly. "How did you know I was here?"

"I saw you from the upstairs window. Are you going to spend the morning feeling sorry for yourself?"

"Is that what I'm doing?" he growled.

"It can be very seductive," she told him. "Tarragon tells me the cause of what she referred to as a 'crack-up' was due to a plane accident. I insisted upon inquiring, and she explained the circumstances."

"She shouldn't have done that," he snapped.

"Nonsense. A little older and wiser, she would know that you only learned how fragile we all are, we human beings, 'mere souls bearing up corpses,' as Epictetus phrased it, and it frightened you."

"It's that simple?" he said sarcastically. "Is that what I learned?"

Her glance was severe. "I find sarcasm very immature," she said coldly, "and my breakfast is waiting. Of course it's not that simple. What it brings with it—" She hesitated. "What follows such a crisis is a depressing and distressing disillusionment."

Startled, he said, "With what?"

"God," she said, and with her ironic smile and a flutter of chiffon she was gone.

"God?" he thought. "*God?*"

She was, of course, a little mad, she had to be. He lay down again, and the sun, inching its way through the towering stalks of corn dissipated the shadows and warmed the earth beneath him; presently he fell asleep, this time without dreams.

Whether it was the sense of a presence, or the sun that woke him, when he opened his eyes again it was to see a woman standing down near the zucchini watching him: salt-and-pepper hair pulled sternly into a ponytail, a handsome tanned face, baggy pants, and an old sweatshirt.

Andrew sat up in astonishment. "*You?*" he gasped.

She left the zucchini to join him, and seated herself companionably on the earth beside him; he couldn't remember her ever doing anything so spontaneous before. She said, "You've entered *my* territory now, Andrew, so if your father learns we've met, you must—absolutely *must*—remind him the agreement applied only to New York." She smiled at him. "Welcome to Tottsville, Andrew."

"Agreement?" he stammered. "Tottsville?"

"Well, you see," she said in the tangential way that he remembered, "your father acted so very embarrassed and secretive about a relative named Harriet Thale that early in our marriage I simply had to find out why."

Andrew suddenly laughed. "You're serious?" It struck him as a joke of cosmic proportions. "You actually met her, then, the shocking aunt Harriet Thale?"

She beamed at him cordially. "Met her and sneaked away from Manhattan as often as I could, and when I left your father, where else would any sensible fugitive come for solace?"

"Orange marmalade!" he cried. "It was *you*. And you live—"

She nodded. "Across the pond."

This was almost too much to absorb at once; he supposed he was in shock at finding his long-gone mother here, of all places. "Pond," he repeated blankly.

"The Bide-A-Wee cottage."

He said incredulously, "Does my father know?"

"Good heavens, of course not!"

He stared at her wonderingly. He blurted out, "You look

happy—you never looked happy before. I remember when I'd come home from summer camp or boarding school you were always knitting. Like Madame Defarge at the guillotine."

She laughed. "And still knit," she told him. "I design and knit outrageous sweaters that sell for outrageous prices in several boutiques in Pittsville, and when they're not selling I paint houses."

"You've become an artist!"

She looked amused. "No, Andrew, I climb up a ladder carrying a bucket of paint and a spray gun and brushes, and paint a house. Manuel's wife and I are partners."

When he looked stunned by this she smiled. "I thought it time to see you, Andrew, and Miss L'Hommedieu said I'd find you here."

"I've been here four days."

"Yes, but when I learned on Saturday you were here I didn't expect you to stay."

He said ruefully, "I didn't expect to stay either."

"Aha," said his mother, "Gussie's worked her magic, has she?"

"Not at all," he said stiffly. "I had a fight with Father, and I'm out of a job now."

"You can't be, I read your books," she told him. "Both of them. Eagerly."

He felt inordinately pleased at this and waited to hear her say that she had been very impressed, or had at least enjoyed them. When she only looked thoughtful, he said accusingly, "You didn't like them."

"I was tremendously proud of you," she said warmly.

"But didn't like them. You can be truthful, I can take it," he said.

She laughed. "No author means that, Andrew. You're *good*, you wrote two very literary and erudite mystery novels, and you certainly caught the Manhattan life that your father gave you—heaven only knows I'm an expert on *that*—and you solved the murders brilliantly." She hesitated. "It was the people, the characters in your books—" She frowned. "I can't easily explain it but—"

He said uneasily, "All that, but *what?*"

"The people in your books were sophisticated but so—so brittle," she said. "They seemed very much alike, and I didn't *like* any of them. I worried about you, Andrew, that your life might be full of people like that, clever and witty but not real. People who cast no shadows."

Cast no shadows!

He realized that he ought to be indignant, hearing this, ought to defend his lost career and certainly mention the three reviewers who had found his books so clever—the word *virtuoso* had even been mentioned—but he was remembering the one maverick review that described his characters as "thin," as having emerged from the author's pen "like cardboard figures given tiresomely flippant remarks to speak."

He said ruefully, "I've been feeling lately that I cast no shadow myself."

She leaned over and kissed him on the cheek. "Nonsense, you were the most affectionate and loving child anyone could have had. Do forgive us both, Andrew—but especially your father, because it's not you he's angry at, you know."

"Then who?"

"Me," she said simply. "Given the evidence that's in front of me—you!—I begin to see that you'll never be another Horace Thale. In fact I suspect you take after me, which must frustrate him terribly." She shook her head and sighed. "And once we were quite happy, you know."

"In those bicycle-repair-shop days," he said dryly.

"He doesn't like that mentioned," she reminded him, with a glance at her watch. "I must go, Linda and I are painting the Witkowski shutters this morning, but Miss L'Hommedieu has promised to show me the will that you miraculously found last night. They're becoming very fond of you, Andrew, and I'm not surprised in the least."

They both rose, but as they passed the zucchini, he said pointedly, "And what was the agreement you mentioned?"

She sighed. "I hate talking about that, it reflects so very badly on my maternal instincts—which I do have, Andrew, truly—but you have to realize I was growing quite desperate."

"The agreement," he repeated firmly.

She nodded. "It was the price of leaving. To allow him to— well, guide you without interference."

"Or mold me?"

"Whatever. Not see you. That and no alimony because I was the one leaving."

Aghast he said, "Not even a dime?"

"Oh no, there was a lump sum of five thousand dollars."

"My God, only five thousand?"

"Quite understandable," she said. "He assumed I would have to come back to him."

"But how did you manage?"

She smiled. "For a year I was one of your great-aunt Harriet's strays. She refused any money, bless her. And then one day the Bide-A-Wee cottage came on the market for the precise sum of five thousand dollars. No insulation, no heat except for a fireplace. But two bedrooms. I bought it. Leo installed a space heater—"

"No doubt stolen from Hobe Elkin," he said, nodding.

"—and Manuel and Linda helped me to insulate it." Stopping by the sunflowers she said, "Do you like Tarragon?"

Taken aback by this abrupt change in direction he said, "Of course, but I think it downright insulting, their advertising for a young man in the newspapers for her."

His mother said with interest, "Do you really? I thought it innocent and very touching."

"Touching!"

"Well, yes. All through high school, you see, Tarragon had a job as a waitress after classes ended—they needed the money, Miss Thale having died. No time for teenage dates *there*! After that she spent a year at the community college in Pittsville on a scholarship—*still* waiting on tables—and this past winter she was a kindergarten aide in town. Most people overlook Tarragon and assume it's Gussie who holds things together—as she does, in many ways—but Leo and Miss L'Hommedieu and Gussie know better. I thought it very sweet of them."

"Oh," he said, thinking what a bloody narcissist he'd been, talking so much about himself.

"And if you *don't* like her," she said crossly, "I will never speak to you again."

Andrew grinned. "I more than like her," he admitted.

He thought his mother chuckled. "Gussie will no doubt take credit for that, of course." She looked up at the sunflowers towering over them. "She really has powers, that woman! Just look at them, they'll soon be as high as the house!"

They sat around the kitchen table, Leo, Tarragon, Miss L'Hommedieu, and Andrew, while his mother brewed tea for them. "Rosemary for remembrance," she said, distributing the cracked china cups.

Gussie was absent, but no one questioned this but Andrew.

"She has gone to the woods," Miss L'Hommedieu told him in a kind voice.

Turning to Leo she said, "Was it Anatole France, Leo, or was it Balzac who wrote that 'Chance is the word that God uses when He wants to remain anonymous'?"

"It was Anatole France," Leo said. "You've got the meaning but the words aren't *quite* right," he told her. "You'll have a story for us this evening?"

Miss L'Hommedieu bowed graciously. "I shall, of course, yes."

It was in this manner that Andrew, without asking, knew that no letter had been found in their search of the house.

His mother, sipping her tea, was scanning the will. "You've

looked everywhere?" she asked of them. "She *wanted* you to find her money, I don't understand why the instructions weren't stapled or clipped to the will. Or included in it."

"I suppose we begin digging now?" said Andrew.

She ignored this, frowning. "I think you must take this to a lawyer—never mind the missing letter—so that Horace, Andrew's father, can be notified that he's not, after all, the owner. A matter of putting first things first." With a last glance at the will she said, "I see that Mr. Branowski witnessed this. That's interesting, don't you think? Is he still in the woods?"

Tarragon nodded. "I took him tea and bread last night. I found him over by Magic Vale."

"Magic Vale?" said Andrew with interest.

"That's *mine*," Tarragon told him with a smile. "It's a perfect fairy ring, at least that's what I thought when I was seven years old, and it's been mine ever since."

"Tarragon," said Andrew's mother, "I think that you should find Mr. Branowski and bring him here to read the will personally, and ask if he can recall any comments that Harriet made at the time."

"But it's been five years," protested Leo. "And he drinks."

"He drinks, but drunk or sober I've never underestimated his intelligence," she said, rising, and to Andrew, "Dig *later*."

And she was gone: to paint shutters, Andrew realized, and found himself grinning at the thought, too diverted to be depressed.

There was a long and thoughtful silence following her departure, and then Tarragon said, "So now we need a lawyer and Mr. Branowski . . . It's been quite a morning."

"Begun at one A.M.," pointed out Andrew.

"Very competent woman, your mother," said Leo. "Find her much changed since you last saw her?"

"Changed?" echoed Andrew. "*Changed?* Any woman last seen wearing Chanel and diamonds who's now a housepainter living in a cottage called Bide-A-Wee has undergone one hell of a change." He smiled. "I like her."

Amused, Tarragon said, "*Like* her?"

"I don't think I ever really knew her at all," he admitted in surprise. "Anyone living with my father seems to have weird things happen to them—he overpowers people."

"And you heard what she said, Gussie," Leo reminded her. "First thing tomorrow you better put on your town clothes and visit a lawyer."

Gussie nodded. "I can do that, yes."

"But first we need a lawyer's name," pointed out Tarragon. "I'll pick the cucumbers for lunch and then take the shortcut to the post office and ask Artemus, he'll know who to see."

"*I* can pick cucumbers," Andrew told her. "How many?"

She flashed him a smile. "Thanks—pick four," and she, too, was gone.

Andrew found the cucumbers in line three, neatly bedded in straw to keep the damp earth from rotting them, and picked four of the sleekest and ripest, and then wandered over to the low-walled herb garden. Almost at once he was assailed by a profusion of scents, but what he had come to find was the herb tarragon. Unfortunately there were no labels to identify any of them, and he recognized only the mints by the fragrance of them. Plucking a leaf he was having a good taste of it when Leo found him.

"So you've found our herbs," Leo said. "Some days the smell of them's almost enough to make a person drunk. I tell you, though, Nature's kind. Most of them grow wild out in the woods and the meadows, ready for anybody's taking."

He seated himself on a corner of the stone wall not pre-empted by a tangle of green leaves, and lifting his face to the sun he nodded. "It's a good sun today for the garden." Regarding the sprig of green in Andrew's hand, "That's spearmint. It's rosemary sunning itself here along the wall. *Likes* walls. And basil's over there, and comfrey—" He pointed to a growth of tall plants bearing purple flowers. "Comfrey's a healing herb for the insides of a person, and for hurts on the outside."

"Where's the tarragon?" asked Andrew.

"Ah," he said, "you're not talking of our Tarragon, you want to see the herb. There," he said of a tall shrub bearing smooth dark green leaves. "Pick a leaf. The sweetest of them all, Miss Thale always said." As Andrew plucked one of its long narrow leaves and held it to his nose Leo chuckled. "So?"

Andrew said slowly, "It smells like—like summer. The sweetness of a summer day."

"Very poetic," Leo said appreciatively. "Unless, of course, you grow up in Hell's Kitchen or the Bowery, like me. It'll be flowering next month, we'll harvest it and hang the stalks to dry in the attic. A pity you won't be here."

Andrew, startled, said, "No, I don't suppose—" But he didn't want to think of that.

"So where are the cucumbers?" inquired Tarragon, suddenly appearing on the other side of the wall, and smiling. "I've gone all the way to the post office and back, and still no cucumbers?"

"He was curious about our herb garden," said Leo.

"Then by all means we must lend him our best two-volume book on herbs," she said mischievously. "And insist he read it."

"Yes, but did Artemus recommend a lawyer?" asked Andrew.

She said triumphantly, "Not only that, but Artemus called him, and Gussie has an appointment tomorrow morning at ten o'clock to see an attorney named Abner Margus in Pittsville."

"Glory be," said Leo, and returned to the house for their lunch of cucumber sandwiches.

That evening when Andrew walked down to the pond, towel in hand, the heat of the day had diminished, and when he shrugged off his jeans and sneakers the air felt deliciously cool on his bare shoulders. A curious silence had descended on the pond, a hush, as if it was intermission and the scenery was being changed, the earth shifting from day to night: a few birdcalls. Crickets. The muted sound of a car on the distant highway. Even the water had stilled and was clear as a mirror until he saw that, over to his right, on the western shore, a cloud of mist was forming low over the pond. As it took shape it began to flow toward him, almost to dance, as the twilight coolness of the coming night met the day's warmth of the pond. It moved with a sinister speed, always

close to the water, sending out fingers of pale cloud, silent
and ghostly.

The water had already cooled when he walked into its shal-
lows, and was cooler yet when he dove into it. Swimming up
from its pebbled bottom he opened his eyes to see that one of
the last rays of sunlight had laced the surface with bright silver; it was dazzling until the mist swept over it, darkening it
into dull pewter.

When he came out of the water he was shivering but exhil-
arated. Wrapping himself in his towel, teeth chattering, he
found a patch of grass still bright with sun on which to warm
himself and sat down, realizing that already—and as usual—
his mind was reaching for words to describe the look of the
pond as it slowly disappeared under that moving blanket of
mist. Words, always words! Obnoxious, obsessive, or wonderful, he was stuck with words . . . Sometimes it pleased him to
think of how storytelling must have begun thousands of years
ago, when a man wearing no more than the skins of an animal
returned from the hunt to sit around a campfire and boast of
his triumphs—making a damn good story of it, he was sure—
even if in gestures and grunts . . . troubadours had sung their
stories . . . priests had written them on parchment. A strange
need, this compulsion to express, and not for artists alone.
People created homes, they created gardens, Harriet Thale
had created a life, his father seemed intent on creating a fortune, but something deep inside of Andrew compelled him
to create stories, and he knew that he would always feel incomplete—restless, too, and deprived—if he could never

again lose himself utterly in the delicious excitement of entering a world carved out of imagination.

He wondered if Miss L'Hommedieu was speaking *his* truth, too, when she'd told Tarragon that she wrote to escape reality. He thought of the unending summer camps and boarding schools he'd been sent to in the past, his father remote, his mother a muted shadow in the background; and could he forget the longing for a real family that at nine or ten he'd poured into his stories; until an implacable anger had chilled him into cynicism? Perhaps it was that anger, that helplessness, that had led him to choose mystery novels to write, because—unlike Miss L'Hommedieu's stories—they had a beginning, a middle and an ending, and murders in a book were more easily solved than the deficiencies in his own life. His plots were neat and clever, but his mother had been right when she found the characters in his books superficial and cynical. They were the only people he'd known.

Why, he wondered, was he seeing this now?

The answer to that was waiting for him, too. There was a family at Thale's Folly, certainly an ill-assorted group of strays, he thought, smiling, but a *family*. And among them was Tarragon, and now his mother.

Abruptly he laughed, because an ant was crawling over his bare leg, no doubt irritated as hell at this long damp obstacle keeping it from its destination, and here he was, sitting on the grass in danger of being discovered by ticks at any moment. What an idiotic place to sit!

He plucked his jeans and sneakers from the beach and set out on the path to the house, past the buttercups and yarrow, the daisies and the Queen Anne's lace. There would be a sunset to watch, and later Miss L'Hommedieu's story-of-the-day to hear; Miss Thale's will had been found, tomorrow Gussie and Leo would visit a lawyer, and in the morning he and Tarragon would look for Mr. Branowski.

They would all of them sleep well this night.

Thursday

8

[Lemon balm] is of so great virtue that though it be but tied
to his sword that hath given the wound it staunches the
blood.   —Pliny

When Andrew awoke the next morning it was with a
sense of satisfaction that surprised him, and he decided it must be due to all the rosemary tea he'd been swill-
ing. Outside his window the birds were carrying on their
usual spirited conversation, the sun was shining, and he'd
slept well. On the negative side, of course—and of late he'd
become gifted in a search for negatives—there were the disappointments that lay ahead for the occupants of Thale's
Folly; it would be a tragedy if Miss Thale's money was never
found and they lost their home.

He frowned over this, realizing the burden this would place
on Tarragon. He had never before experienced a need to protect anyone except himself, but there it was, a new emotion
to surprise him.

Thoughtfully he considered his own situation. In his savings account he had managed to preserve—from the advances
on his two published books—an amount that would sound

like wealth to the occupants of Thale's Folly, but in Manhattan would support him for no more than twelve months. He had carefully saved this money for the year or more he would need to write his next novel, and he had accepted help from his father only so that he needn't touch it. Now there was not going to be a next book, and it was time he accepted this; he was going to have to find a nine-to-five job. This was not promising because he had only two years of college to record on a résumé, whereas friends of his who had accumulated B.A.'s and even more prestigious degrees were doing no more than managing shoe stores, fast-food shops, or the selling of ties in Bloomingdale's. Too many good jobs had moved overseas.

More rosemary tea was obviously becoming a necessity to cheer him; he thought it might be interesting to talk to his mother, who appeared to have garnered wisdom that she might share more tactfully than his father. He dressed and went downstairs.

In the kitchen Gussie was slicing bread, wearing an apron over a beige silk dress, a straw hat firmly affixed to her head. "So's I can get used to it," she explained. "Leo and I leave on the eighty-thirty bus to see Mr. Margus, and Artemus is going to drive us to the bus stop before the post office opens."

"Can I help?"

She nodded. "You can butter the bread and fetch the marmalade from the pantry while I finish brewing the tea."

"You're sure you've all the documents, the deed, the map, and the will?"

"All in my purse," she told him, and nodded to Leo as he joined them, wearing a suit that implied a once-bulkier Leo before he met with breakfasts of bread and tea. She was just pouring the tea when a sleek and shining van with four-wheel drive bumped its way up the driveway and came to a stop. This was not Artemus's mail jeep. Inscribed on its door panels were the words BEAR & CRUMBULL, REALTORS.

Andrew, seeing it, said, "Oh no, he wouldn't—he *couldn't!*"

"Wouldn't what?" asked Leo.

"My father's already sent that developer to look over the property."

"Isn't his," Leo pointed out. "Got a will now to prove it."

Gussie, emerging from the pantry, gave Andrew a questioning glance. "Do we tell him?"

"No," Andrew said indignantly. "Let the man see it and price it and want it first. What's important is your getting to the lawyer and making it official."

With a nod toward the stranger climbing out of his van, she said, "You'll deal with it?"

"Gladly," agreed Andrew, and strolled out to confront the man.

With a stern look Mr. Jasper Crumbull handed him his business card. "Here to look over the property of Mr. Horace Thale," he said. In spite of the heat of the day he was wearing a plaid wool vest and a tweed jacket with leather elbow patches but he did not quite succeed in presenting the image of a country squire that he apparently aspired to, being stout, red-faced, and very hot.

Andrew waved a careless hand toward the woods. "You have a map, of course."

"Of course—faxed to me this morning." He eyed Andrew with curiosity. "That way?" he said, pointing.

"That way," Andrew assured him gravely, and watched Mr. Crumbull set out across the untilled field toward the woods, where he would soon lose his way, of this Andrew could be certain. He returned to the kitchen in a cheerful mood, looking forward to the unpleasant surprise that lay in wait for Mr. Crumbull of Bear & Crumbull, Realtors.

Artemus arrived promptly in his mail jeep, and Gussie, nervously clutching her bag and adjusting her hat, was helped into the jeep. Once she and Leo had gone it was necessary to establish Miss L'Hommedieu in her throne-like chair on the side porch before he and Tarragon could look for Mr. Branowski, and this meant equipping her with notebook and pen, several books, and a cup of hot sage tea.

"Bring him back so he can't get away," she counseled them tartly. "It's Gussie who'll want to hear anything he has to say, and Mr. Branowski has a restless spirit."

"Let's just hope we find him—I couldn't, yesterday," pointed out Tarragon, and to Andrew, "Let's first try where you saw him boiling eggs, that's his favorite tree."

"I take it you share my mother's faith in Mr. Branowski's memory?" he said as they set out down the path.

"To be honest, no—after five years? But it's clever of your mother to think of it."

"You mean it inspires hope . . . I'm going to visit Bide-A-

Wee tonight or tomorrow, but Tarragon, can you think of *any-where* my great-aunt could have buried her money? Some corner or place she was partial to? Bald Hill, for instance, or near—er—Gussie's shrine?"

Tarragon shook her head. "None of us can, I wish *I* could but I can't, darn it . . . Here we are, there's his tree."

But Mr. Branowski was not to be found there, although his knapsack hung from a branch of the tree and his bedroll was neatly rolled up at its base. Frowning, Tarragon said, "He wanders, we'll just have to keep looking."

"Where *does* one go when homeless?" asked Andrew.

Tarragon laughed. "Did you think he has no social life? According to Artemus, the population of Tottsville in the winter is six hundred fifty but in the summer it's almost three thousand, counting children, and everyone knows Mr. Branowski by now. He's considered one of Tottsville's 'characters.' He sometimes visits Manuel," she said, "and he often poses for one of the artists, or he scavenges for bottle money, or—just disappears." She frowned. "He's—well, Mr. Branowski. Let's try the pond next."

The pond was placid in the afternoon heat, the sun scattering sequin-like glitter across its surface. Andrew thought that a swim would be a wonderful way to spend the next hour but he acceded to the importance of finding Mr. Branowski and so they stood on the beach, scanning the shoreline and the woods that edged it until suddenly the quiet was shattered by a man's voice shouting, "Help, help! Police!"

Mr. Crumbull of Bear & Crumbull stumbled out of the

underbrush, his face an alarming red. "Thank God," he gasped at sight of them. "There's a man—they threw him out of a car, I saw it. I think he's dead."

"Dead?" said Andrew blankly.

"You mean really *dead*?" said Tarragon.

"I don't know, he just lies there. It was terrible—they drove past and just opened the door and—I swear they *kicked* him out of the car." Mr. Crumbull was perspiring profusely. "Thank God they didn't see me! Call the police!"

Tarragon turned to Andrew. "Find Artemus," she said quickly. "I'll go back with Mr. Crumbull and flag you down on the road when we get there. You *can* take me back to him, Mr. Crumbull?"

"I feel sick," he said, clutching his stomach.

Rallying, Andrew told him curtly, "Be sick later," and with a nod to Tarragon, "What's the shortest way?"

She pointed. "Take that path around the pond, jump over the brook, keep straight and you'll meet the highway near the garage, and if Artemus is still delivering mail bring Manuel, he's deputy sheriff."

But Andrew had already begun running. It was a long way, and when he reached the highway he was in as bad a shape as Mr. Crumbull, dripping sweat and out of breath.

Manuel, adjusting a carburetor, looked up in surprise.

"Dead man," panted Andrew. "Woods. Mr. Crumbull the realtor found him. Says he was thrown out of a car."

"Is that so," Manuel said, and lifting his voice bellowed, "Junior? Junior!"

Manuel Junior emerged from the dark interior of the garage. "Yeah? What's up, Pop?"

"Lock up the garage and find Artemus. Dead man in the woods." And to Andrew, "Hop in my truck."

"Why can't I see the dead man, too?" complained Junior.

"You see enough of them on television," his father told him, climbing into the cab beside Andrew. "Where do we go?"

"Tarragon said she'd flag us down when she finds the place."

Manuel nodded, placed his foot on the accelerator, and they shot off with the speed of a catapult. Tarragon, just seating herself on a rock next to the road, waved at sight of them and then vanished. Bringing the truck to a halt they jumped out to discover that she was helping Mr. Crumbull to his feet; he had taken Andrew's advice to be sick later, and had been very sick indeed among the ferns.

As for Mr. Crumbull's dead man he was lying on the ground with his eyes open, staring blankly at the sky above him.

"*Not* dead," said Andrew in relief.

Manuel stared down at the man in astonishment. Pointing a grease-stained finger at him he said, "Damned if he's not the man who was always hanging around my garage looking for you, Andrew."

Andrew said in protest, "He can't be."

"He certainly is."

Tarragon gasped, "Then he's the man who broke into—" At a warning glance from Manuel she said weakly, "—who wanted his raincoat."

A shaken Mr. Crumbull said accusingly, "He reeks of liquor, smell him. Although I'm relieved he's not *dead*," he added piously. "But if you'd seen him thrown out of the car—!"

Manuel, kneeling beside the man, was running his hands over his body, searching for broken bones. They watched as he cautiously lifted one arm and then the other, examined his wrists, legs, and ankles, and gently lifted his head slightly from the ground. Sitting back on his heels he said, "Beats all he's alive. You say he was thrown out of a car?"

"Black Chevrolet," said Mr. Crumbull.

Andrew said, "It's a miracle he's alive."

"The liquor's the miracle," said Manuel. "He's so full of it he just rolled with the punches, probably didn't feel a thing, relaxed as a baby." He addressed the man sternly. "Can you sit up?"

The man's eyes opened again and fastened on Manuel without expression; he frowned, considering the suggestion, struggled to raise himself, immediately clutched his head, groaned, and fell back in a faint.

Manuel nodded. "Hangover or concussion, he's gone unconscious on us. Let's see if we can find out who he is." Manuel's hands slid into the man's pockets and out again, and he shook his head. "They stripped the guy clean." His eyes narrowing with thought he stood up and regarded the man with a frown. "The way I see it—if he was thrown out of a car with murderous intent, then he's supposed to be dead."

"He certainly *should* be," said Mr. Crumbull testily. "They *kicked* him out, I saw it. And the car must have been going fifty miles an hour."

Manuel looked at Mr. Crumbull measuringly. "You sure they didn't see you? I'd appreciate knowing just where you were when that car passed."

Mr. Crumbull obliged. "Sitting on the ground back there, my back against a tree while I jotted down notes." He pointed. "I was figuring out how many Swiss chalets would fit into what I'd seen so far."

"Swiss chalets, eh?" said Manuel, and gave Tarragon an interested glance. "Well, I think if you know what's good for you, then you'll not mention what you've seen here while you were planning all those Swiss chalets. A lot healthier for you."

"Oh my God," said Mr. Crumbull, "am I going to have to go to court to be a witness to this?"

"For the moment, no," said Manuel. "This man is dead. Somebody wanted him dead, they tossed him out of a car and he's dead. You get my point?"

"Not—not quite," stammered Mr. Crumbull. "That is, you don't mean—?"

"I mean," said Manuel patiently, "if you talk about this to anybody—and I mean *anybody*—the news could get back to the guys who threw this man out of the car, and they'd learn our friend is *not* dead. And you could be next."

"Oh my God."

"But if you can keep your mouth shut—"

"Oh I can, I will."

Manuel nodded. "If you can do that then you can go, but first give me your name, address, and phone number so I can find you again if needed."

With a trembling hand Mr. Crumbull presented his business card to Manuel, turned and stumbled away through the underbrush; they were silent until the last of his footsteps died away.

Andrew said, "What are you thinking?"

"Yes," said Tarragon, "and did you have to scare the poor man like that?"

"Yes, if this is as important as I think. Anyway, no need for Mr. Crumbull to be a witness," Manuel said. "We got one right here, and since I can't find any bones broken I say hide him."

"Hide him!" gasped Tarragon.

Manuel nodded. "For a day at least. I got a plan—one I *think* Artemus would agree to. This man stays dead until he can explain those keys to Artemus that you found in his coat, and tell us, and the state police, who threw him out of the car. In a word, testify to certain matters Artemus suspects."

"Like what?"asked Tarragon.

"Like maybe that million-dollar robbery three weeks ago at the Pittsville Bank and Trust . . . Artemus and the state police are sure those keys must belong to a safe deposit box."

Andrew said eagerly, "He was in Connecticut, just over the border, when I took his raincoat by mistake."

"There you are . . . out of state. Figures. Smart, too. Stash the million in a legal safe deposit box until the hunt cools down." Turning to Tarragon he said, "I say we hide him for tonight until he can talk. Really *hide* him, he's got value. You ever met Bill Watson?"

Tarragon frowned. "He's one of the summer people, isn't he?"

Manuel nodded. "Also a doctor. He just might come and look over this chap if we keep him close by. Bill owes me a favor."

"Close by?" said Tarragon.

Manuel grinned. "You got a parlor free, I seem to remember. Or the cellar? Maybe even the attic?"

Tarragon looked doubtful.

"Look," Manuel said, "no sense driving him over the bumps on Thale Road, just in case there's a concussion, and if we go up the highway somebody might see him. We can carry him to Thale's Folly through the woods, me and Andrew here. Keep him safe. We don't want him killed again, you know."

"True," said Tarragon. "Okay, let's go."

Manuel brought from his overalls pocket a wrinkled garage receipt, scribbled a few words on it, and handed it to Andrew with his car keys. "Stick this on my windshield, will you? It tells Artemus where to find me, then move my truck down the road apiece, just in case."

"In case what?"

"In case his friends drive back to make sure he's *really* dead. No point in leaving X marks the spot."

When this had been done, Manuel slung the victim over his broad shoulders and they made their way slowly back through the woods to the house, Andrew clearing the lower branches of sumac to make way for him.

Miss L'Hommedieu, still seated on the side porch, watched their approach with interest, mildly startled to see Manuel and even more startled when she noted the burden he carried. Graciously she rose to open the screen door for them.

"Drinking again, is he?" she said, and Andrew remembered they'd left her to look for Mr. Branowski.

Manuel headed for the kitchen table and deposited their mystery man among the remains of their breakfast.

Miss L'Hommedieu, following them, said indignantly, "That's not Mr. Branowski, you've got the wrong man!"

"This one's your burglar," Manuel said, and sat down to catch his breath.

"He was thrown out of a car," Tarragon told her eagerly. "The real estate man, Mr. Crumbull, actually saw it happen."

Andrew, vigorously nodding his head, added, "And Manuel wants him hidden so they won't know he's still alive."

"Doesn't *look* alive," said Miss L'Hommedieu, and with a sharp glance at Manuel, "Will someone get Manuel a drink of water before the poor man expires?" While this was being accomplished she continued her inspection of the man. "Has a weak chin," she announced, "and a broken nose, too. Just the sort of man they'd throw out of a car. Bungled the job, didn't he? Where do you plan to put him?"

"Cellar?" suggested Manuel.

"Nothing in the cellar to lay him on," said Miss L'Hommedieu. "Try the sofa in the parlor, nobody goes there, but open the windows, he smells to high heaven of whiskey."

The sliding doors to the parlor were opened. The room was stifling, and smelled of moth balls; there was a Persian rug on the floor and a mantel displaying a collection of china angels, but no chair looked comfortable, and after one glance at the sofa, with its ornately carved arms and brocade, they placed the man on the floor. Andrew found a cushion to put under his head, and struggled to open two stubborn windows.

They left him, closing the parlor doors carefully behind them until Artemus could join them.

He arrived ten minutes later. "Same man is he?" was his first question.

"Same man."

Artemus nodded. "That does it—*has* to be a local job or they'd have been a hell of a lot more imaginative about where to dump him. They needed woods? No woods in Pittsville . . . Tottsville has woods? They brought him to Tottsville."

"Who did?"

"*He'll* tell us," Artemus said, nodding at the man on the floor. "I've got my own suspicions, but suspicions don't count in a courtroom. Dear God but he reeks."

"It's my opinion," said Manuel, "they not only filled his insides with whiskey but poured it over him. It's thanks to what was inside him he landed like a cat."

"Which may occur to them, too," mused Artemus, frowning. "I've got a friend on the Pittsville *Gazette*, Tom Bower. I might just ask him to put a line or two in the newspaper tomorrow reporting an unidentified dead man found in these woods. That should reassure his killers."

This was agreed upon. "But don't leave those windows open," Artemus counseled. "If your unexpected guest sobers up during the night he's likely to climb right through them and get away. I'll be back first thing in the morning to take a statement from him; he should be alert by then."

The windows were closed and locked, and their mystery man was left to regain his sobriety among the china angels. Artemus and Manuel drove away, and Miss L'Hommedieu, Tarragon, and Andrew were left to await the return of Gussie and Leo from Pittsville.

9

Sage is singularly good for the head and brain, it
quickeneth the senses and memory, strengtheneth the
sinews, restoreth health to those that have the palsy and
taketh away shakey trembling of the members.
                                    —John Gerard, *The Herball*, 1597

"It's no use," said Gussie, sinking into a chair on their
return at half-past eleven. She looked alarmingly hot,
discouraged, and very tired.

Leo patted her on the shoulder and said, "Now, now, Gussie," and sat down, too.

Tarragon, her eyes wide with concern, said, "What's wrong?
What happened, Gussie? Did you like Mr. Margus? Is the will
legal?"

Andrew was so shocked by Gussie's appearance that without thinking about it he lit the kerosene stove, put water on
to boil, and measured spoonfuls of rosemary into the teapot,
completely unaware that he'd never even approached the
stove before. "What *is* it?" he asked.

"Money," growled Leo.

"Money?" echoed Tarragon.

127

"You'll need cups," Miss L'Hommedieu reminded Andrew sternly.

Gussie nodded. "Money. Mr. Margus made calls about the taxes—eight hundred dollars a year Andrew's father paid—which comes to four thousand dollars for five years and will have to be repaid him, and it's going to take weeks for probate—whatever that is—and although Mr. Margus said he'd charge very little for his services—he was *very* kind—he charges by the hour, and it's obvious he'll have quite a lot of legal work, what with untangling things and filing the will, and—"

"—and we don't have the money," Leo finished for her.

"He said," continued Gussie, looking dispirited, "that we could sell most of the land and keep the house. The house and maybe an acre or two, meaning we'd not have to move, but . . ." Her voice trailed away forlornly.

Swiss chalets, thought Andrew. No pond, no Magic Vale, no pentacles on a stone bench in the woods, the trees cut down, the road paved. Noise. People. Cars. No meadow of blueberries—and the birds? He felt sickened by the thought.

The water was boiling, and Tarragon rose to finish what he'd begun, her face clouded. Andrew said fiercely, "We've got to start digging, that's all. Her will insists there's money somewhere, we've got to start digging."

No one appeared to hear him. "How about a metal detector?" he said, struck by the thought. "We could surely find one somewhere. They detect metal, and gold is metal."

Miss L'Hommedieu was wiser than he: she simply changed the subject. "I think you should know," she announced, "that we harbor a fugitive in the parlor. One might say that astonishing events have occurred while you were gone."

"Events?" said Gussie blankly.

"Fugitive!" exclaimed Leo, eyes brightening.

Miss L'Hommedieu nodded. "A fugitive from the law, as well as from a vicious gang who wanted him dead. It seems he was thrown out of a car bathed in whiskey—"

"Wow," murmured Leo happily.

"—and until he becomes conscious and talks, and until Artemus decides what to do with him, we are hiding him."

"But—who is he?" faltered Gussie.

"He's our burglar," explained Tarragon. "You can open the parlor door and look at him but he's still unconscious."

"Well, *that* gives us something else to think about," Leo pointed out in relief. "Eh, Gussie?" with a worried glance at her.

Tarragon rose from her chair to say, "I'm going to go out and look for Mr. Branowski again."

"And I," said Andrew thoughtfully, "am going to go and see my mother."

"Sweet," said Miss L'Hommedieu approvingly, and turned her attention to comforting Gussie.

He and Tarragon parted at Manuel's garage, where she planned to interrogate him as to where Mr. Branowski might be found. Andrew, however, turned to the right and strolled down the road past Rest-A-Wile and Sunset Roost until he reached the track that led up a graveled path to Bide-A-Wee.

A *far cry from Manhattan*, he thought, viewing the small

cottage with interest: weathered gray shingles, shutters painted white, but—and he smiled—a flaming-red door. He knocked vigorously, hoped that she was at home, and was surprised by his delight when the door opened.

"Andrew," she murmured, "come in. Just back from a painting job. Give me a minute with turpentine and a rag and I'll be with you."

"I want to talk to you," he said. "*Need* to."

"Good." She pointed to a tiny kitchen. "There's iced tea in the refrigerator, you can pour us two glasses."

But Andrew was staring at the living room, which was outrageously colorful: a purple ceiling with three fake white beams; a peacock chair painted orange, a barrel chair painted yellow, a fireplace with a woodstove in front of it whose pipe went up the chimney; a tubular metal structure in one corner, filled with skeins of bright wool; a sagging couch and a table, next to the window overlooking the lake, on which she apparently drew her sweater designs.

"Awesome," he said, looking around him. "Really wild."

She emerged from the kitchen, wiping her hands on a rag, and seeing that he'd not approached the refrigerator she went back and returned with two glasses of iced tea. "No more Bloomingdale's," she said with a smile. "Garage sales, flea markets, and thrift shops. Have a seat, Andrew."

He said, "Gussie and Leo saw the lawyer this morning—"

She nodded. "I saw them waiting for the bus."

"—and came home terribly discouraged. There are lawyer fees, probate fees, inheritance taxes, my father to repay, and little hope of finding Miss Thale's money. The lawyer's suggested a solution. He pointed out they could sell twenty-two or twenty-three acres and still keep the house."

"Yes," said his mother, watching him with interest.

"What I want to know," he said, "is do you think they'd accept that and stay? I mean, it will probably break their hearts to lose so much, but would they *stay*? Without the woods and the pond and Gussie's altar, and hedged in by Swiss chalets? If, of course, they can sell most of the land. I have to know what you think."

"Yes, I see that," she said, amused. "Won't you sit down?"

He sat down. "I'm sitting. What's your opinion?"

"My opinion," she said, "is that Gussie, Leo and Miss L'Hommedieu know a great deal about compromise, Andrew, far more than you or I have known. Where would they go? Of course they'd stay. Is that all you came to ask?"

He suddenly relaxed and grinned. "Of course not. Among other things, would you happen to know where a metal detector could be found?"

"Hmmm," she murmured. "Brown's Rent-A-Tool would probably have one. But there's more on your mind than that, isn't there?" When he nodded sheepishly she smiled. "I thought so."

"You've become psychic," he told her, and proceeded to explain exactly what was on his mind. In detail.

When he had finished, she glanced at her watch and said, "It's twelve-thirty, and there's a bus into Pittsville in fifteen minutes, we can just make it if we hurry. I'll go with you, you'd never find the place. Have you money with you?"

"I didn't expect—" He took out his wallet and examined its contents. "Only seven dollars and my credit card, but I can hurry back to the house and get my checkbook and—"

"And miss the bus?" his mother said, smiling. "Credit cards are beloved by all these days, and I can—what is the word—give you countenance?"

Having promised secrecy about their mysterious man in the parlor he said, "They might wonder why I've disappeared."

"With all they have to worry about? Nonsense," she told him. "Let's go. We'll have to run, too, it grows late."

When Andrew returned to Thale's Folly he found they had delayed dinner for him, and he was touched by their waiting. Gussie, looking less tired now, gave him an appreciative glance. "I see you had a really good visit with your mother."

"Oh a very good one," he said, which was certainly true. "Actually we took the bus into town. I've rented a metal detector, it's outside on the porch." It had been the least of his errands, but he did not feel it time to mention the more important one.

"Metal detector!" gasped Leo. "Andrew, you really think—?"

"Why not? They use it on beaches to find coins that were lost and buried in the sand. We can try it out tonight before it gets dark."

Gussie, suddenly radiant, said, "We might begin on the big field by the side porch, don't you think?"

"We can put stakes in the ground at each end," Tarragon said eagerly. "Six or seven inches apart so we can move in straight lines and not repeat ourselves. Andrew, how clever of you!"

He tried to look appropriately modest, but considering the crises of varying degrees they'd been plunged into over the past twenty-four hours, he changed the subject by asking what had happened while he was away.

"You missed the doctor," Gussie said dryly. "Manuel smuggled him in with the greatest secrecy. You'd have thought hundreds of people were watching."

"City man," growled Leo contemptuously, "but nice enough."

"Concussion?" asked Andrew.

"Very mild. Mainly shock and liquor," said Miss L'Hommedieu disapprovingly. "We were advised to remove him from the Persian rug because he may vomit later."

"But not necessarily," put in Gussie.

"He's to be kept very quiet," added Tarragon, "while he—as the doctor put it—'sleeps it off.'"

Leo gave Gussie a grin. "And Gussie has just the antidote for him when he wakes up and can keep it down."

"Yes I remember," Andrew said wryly. "Dump night."

"The doctor thought it a miracle the man being alive, too."

"Which means," said Miss L'Hommedieu, nodding, "that he has been preserved for mysterious and important reasons."

"Like more burglaries?" quipped Andrew, but was quelled by Miss L'Hommedieu's reproachful glance.

Tarragon had made their dinner, "because Gussie's tired from her trip this morning," she said, tactfully avoiding the word *depressed*. It was a vegetable stew in which Andrew counted potato, onions, kale, green beans, parsley, and spinach, with a touch of garlic—all grown in their garden, which impressed him, and dessert was a custard. A *virtual banquet*, thought Andrew. Once they had finished, they hurried out to the porch to inspect the metal detector that leaned against Miss L'Hommedieu's chair. They would take turns, said Leo, looking it over, but he would go first because he had the most muscle—and looking at his broad shoulders Andrew thought that yes he did. Tarragon brought sticks from the woodpile, Gussie contributed string, and Andrew helped them to stake out the lines down which they should move, while Leo, given this new toy, began at once on the farthest end. He moved slowly, like a farmer sowing seed, the handle gripped firmly with both hands, and Andrew realized that what he had contributed today was not only a metal detector, but hope. He was sure of this when Gussie excused herself and without explanation headed into the woods, to her emerald-green mossy retreat, but she returned in time to watch the sun set.

"And now Miss L'Hommedieu's story," announced Tarragon. "Can't miss hearing *that*."

Twilight had faded into darkness; it was a comforting return to normalcy to gather around the kitchen table and be entertained by Miss L'Hommedieu. Two candles had been lit; a soft warm breeze reached them through the opened windows, bringing with it the scent of warm earth and the sound of crickets. The light of the candle turned Tarragon's eyes a brilliant sapphire and rested kindly on the rough, craggy features of Leo's face. As for Miss L'Hommedieu, in flowing chiffon tonight, Andrew thought that she looked exactly like an ancient priestess.

From the folds of chiffon she brought out a sheet of paper, and clearing her throat began to read: " 'There is no way of knowing how or why, but, somewhere in the hills, a young girl wanders wild and free in the land she loved as a child. Miracles, like people,' " she read, " 'can never be dissected or analyzed or captured in a bottle, and if it was true that she was a ghost—that she'd been killed by a jealous lover—she was nevertheless seen on moonlit nights as clearly as if she was flesh and blood.' "

She stopped, and there was silence. It occurred to Andrew for the first time that each fragment, each vignette that she wrote was bestowed upon them like a gift that each of them could finish in their own way. For Andrew her story brought back to him the ghostly mist that he'd watched creep over the pond the evening before, and in the flickering light of the candles he could believe in that ghost, wandering free and wild among the hills.

Until, with a wry smile, he recalled that a very un-ghostlike burglar lay drunk in their parlor, safely removed from the Persian rug lest he vomit, and this brought him back to the moment.

Friday

10

Thou pretty herb of Venus' tree,
Thy true name it is Yarrow;
Now who my bosom friend must be,
Pray tell thou me to-morrow.   —Halliwell, *Popular Rhymes*

Andrew, waking early, hurried to dress so that he could continue the search of the field for his great-aunt's money. *Like hunting pirate treasure*, he thought whimsically. It was just six o'clock when he tiptoed up the hall to the rarely used front staircase and descended to quietly open one of the sliding doors to the parlor and see how their burglar had fared during the night. He was surprised to see that Leo was fast asleep on the sofa while their mystery man, still on the floor, snored loudly. Closing the door, Andrew walked down the hall into the kitchen and found Artemus seated at the table with a thermos in front of him, his mail jeep visible beyond the open door.

He nodded companionably at Andrew. "Brought coffee with me, not being herbal. Care for a cup?"

"I'd love some," Andrew said fervently. But you're certainly early!"

Artemus poured his thick, fragrant, steaming brew into a china cup and handed it to him. "I'll be waking up the chap in the parlor shortly, I'm here to tape-record a statement from him before I go to work. If he talks, and says what I hope he'll say, there'll be some arrests by the state police today. After that your overnight guest will be tucked away in jail as a witness." With a nod toward the open door he added, "Gussie let me in. She's doing whatever witches do in the woods."

Curious, Andrew said, "You really believe, then, that she's a witch?"

Artemus considered this seriously. "One has to admit she *knows* things."

"Like what?" asked Andrew, sipping coffee he'd not tasted for five days.

Artemus chuckled. "You've seen her sunflowers. And even in a drought it's spooky how her vegetables thrive. She certainly saved Mr. Branowski when he had pneumonia and the Pittsville doctor said he was a goner. It's a strange power she seems to have."

"You do think she's a witch, then?"

"I look at it this way," Artemus said thoughtfully. "I'm not good with words, but she has—well, I'd call it an uncanny connection—a kinship—with Nature. That's as far as I'd go, but your great-aunt Miss Thale said Gussie comes from a long line of such people—probably burned at the stake in the old days—so she's inherited whatever it is." He frowned. "Which is why I hate like hell this news about losing the house, woods, and pond to Swiss chalets. I think Miss Gussie Pease would just fade away."

"I think so, too," said Andrew.

Artemus put down his cup of coffee and brought out a thick notebook, a pen, and his tape recorder. "Time to get to work. Strictly private, Leo'll have to leave the parlor; he stayed the night there."

Artemus disappeared, and Leo appeared and volunteered to make breakfast while Andrew advanced their work on the field with the metal detector. When he came in again, Gussie had returned from the woods, breakfast was waiting and Miss L'Hommedieu was making a stately entrance, followed by Tarragon.

"Half the field's been gone over now—nothing yet," he said, wiping the sweat from his forehead. "Going to be another hot day."

"We could finish the field by noon, couldn't we?" asked Tarragon. "If we still find nothing we can start on the front, and then around the side porch, and—" She made a face at what she was saying and retrenched. "We're sure to find it, and I insist on detecting next, before I go look for Mr. Branowski again."

"No clues yesterday?" asked Andrew.

She shook her head. "Nobody's even *seen* him."

They looked up as Artemus walked into the kitchen carrying his tape recorder and looking pleased. "He's talked," he told them. "Name's Albert Griggs, left New York City six weeks ago and ended up jobless in Pittsville."

Startled, Andrew said, "But you thought a gang?"

He nodded. "Oh yes, Cal Merkle's gang of young hoodlums. Break-ins usually, small stuff. Seems they got ambitious and planned that bank robbery, and damn it, lucked into nearly a million . . . Didn't think Cal had the brains for it. Apparently he met Griggs in a bar in Pittsville, and Griggs must have looked a godsend to him. A new face from out of town, owned a suit and broke, very broke. Took him on as driver and bagman."

"Bagman?" echoed Gussie.

"Bagman. And the bank where Griggs rented the safe-deposit box was the Connecticut Savings and Loan." With a glance at his watch Artemus said, "Post office opens in three minutes, got to go." With a nod he left, and they listened to the sound of his jeep as it backed out of the driveway and drove away.

Gussie said firmly, "If the man's awake, take him that glass of juice, Leo, and Andrew, cut a slice of bread for him, too, will you?"

Andrew followed Leo into the parlor, bearing his slice of bread on a plate. Mr. Griggs was still lying on the floor, his eyes closed following his ordeal with Artemus, but he looked more exhausted than asleep. Leo stood over him, glass in hand, and said gruffly, "Got something to make you feel better, but you'll have to sit up."

The man stirred and opened his eyes, stared up at the ceiling, then lowered his gaze to Andrew's face and shifted his glance to Leo.

Abruptly his eyes widened, and he said wonderingly, "*Leo?*"

There was a moment of shocked silence before an astonished Andrew said, "He knows you?"

"Never saw him before in my life," Leo told him indignantly.

Griggs looked around the room with curiosity. "But where—where am I?"

Andrew said sternly, "You're in the house you burgled two nights ago, leaving my room in a god-awful mess."

"But"—his gaze returned to Leo—"still here?" He struggled to sit up and at once gasped, "My head!" and clutched it with both hands.

Educated by Hobe Elkins's blackberry brandy, and knowing exactly how he must feel, Andrew said, "Give him the hellish brew, Leo."

Handing him the glass, Griggs took a sip, his eyes still on Leo, puzzled. He shuddered as Gussie's antidote hit him, gagged, gasped, and then emptied the glass, but when he handed it back to Leo, the color was already returning to his strained white face.

The door slid open and Miss L'Hommedieu swept into the room to assess the situation, and standing next to Leo looked down at the man with interest.

Griggs said incredulously, "You too?"

"What's this all about?" demanded Leo. "He thinks he *knows* me—and now *you*?"

"He appears too sober to be hallucinating," said Miss L'Hommedieu and leaned over to study his face with scholarly interest. "His hair is obviously dyed black—and very badly. I have often suspected that a beard can hide a weak chin," she added calmly. "If you picture him with a beard and a mustache, Leo—a very *sweeping* mustache—and the nose not broken . . . Look at his eyes, Leo, and those eyebrows and cheekbones."

Leo stared at the man, scowling, and abruptly said, "My God, not *Hamlet*?"

Mr. Griggs groaned. " 'A man whom Fortune hath cruelly scratched—' "

"*Taming of the Shrew*," said Miss L'Hommedieu, nodding. "Definitely Hamlet," and added gently, "Welcome to Thale's Folly, Hamlet."

Andrew decided they had both gone a little mad until he saw the tears running down the man's cheeks. "I left New York—*desperate* to find you," he gasped. "I hoped—so hoped—but there was no lawn and no croquet set, the grass so high, paint peeling off the house—I thought it empty, and—" His voice broke in a sob and he scrubbed at his tears with dirty hands. "I've found you—after all?" he said, and hiccuped.

"Miss Thale is dead," Miss L'Hommedieu told him in a kind voice, "but Gussie is still here, and Leo, and Tarragon."

"Little Tarragon," he repeated. "Oh my God."

"Not so little," said Leo, and raising his voice he shouted, "Gussie? Gussie!"

"But who is he?" asked Andrew.

"One of Harriet's strays . . . an actor. Or was," replied Miss L'Hommedieu, and extended a hand to him. "See if you can stand up—you're Mr. Griggs now, are you?"

He tottered to his feet and promptly sank down on the sofa. "It seemed a good name," he muttered, and more urgently, "What happened to me? They gave me three days to find those bank keys—" Tears of weakness spilled from his eyes. "If I couldn't find those keys they said—they said—"

"They did," said Andrew. "Threw you out of a car drunk and reeking with whiskey."

"Yet here I am at Thale's Folly! If only—*only* I'd known you were here! I hitchhiked up from New York, no job, no money, no prospects, and—"

"And got into very bad company," pointed out Leo.

"I hadn't eaten in two days, I'd hoped Miss Thale would take me in."

Andrew said to Leo, "But didn't you know his name? recognize the name Griggs?"

Miss L'Hommedieu said tartly, "Scarcely possible when seven years ago—it *is* seven years, isn't it?—he was Toby Gravino."

The sliding doors flew open and Gussie, followed by Tarragon, said crossly, "What is it now, Leo, we were busy—"

"It's Hamlet," Leo told her.

"Hamlet?" gasped Tarragon. "Oh Mr. Gravino, I've never forgotten you, how wonderful to see you again!"

"You'll have him crying again," pointed out Miss L'Hommedieu. "He's very weak just now."

Gussie said sharply, "All very well to welcome him, but he broke into this house—how *could* you, Hamlet!"

"I never dreamed it was *you* still living here . . ."

"No croquet set," Andrew explained dryly.

"I thought—long gone," he said, and added miserably, " 'Oh, what a world of vile ill-favored faults!' . . . That man— that man who asked all those questions, I'm to go to jail now?"

"Yes," said Andrew.

"Oh no," cried Tarragon.

"You've grown up," he said in a dazed voice, staring at her. "You've grown beautiful."

" 'They that touch pitch will be defiled,' " pointed out Miss L'Hommedieu.

He nodded. *Much Ado About Nothing.* Yes, of course to jail I must go. A new experience for me at least—'there's small choice in rotten apples!' but—'Ah, the inaudible and noiseless foot of Time!' "

Tarragon grinned at Andrew mischievously. "Mr. Gravino is how I learned Shakespeare, he hasn't changed a bit."

"Yes, he fairly drips it," said Andrew. "What do we do now?"

"I know what *I* do," said Gussie. "It's my turn to run the machine over the field. Two more rows to do, and if that *thing* doesn't find"—with a glance at Hamlet—"doesn't find you-know-what, we'll know nothing is buried there. Unfortunately."

"Lawn mowing, is it?" said Hamlet. "Give me an hour or two, and I'll help. Penance," he added. "A trifle frail just now, but if I'm to sit in a jail cell for weeks"—he sighed—" 'to be imprisoned in the viewless winds, and blown with restless violence 'round about the pendant world . . .' "

Gussie patted him on the shoulder. "Just rest, Mr. Gravino, and enjoy being alive. What you need is some red clover tea to clear your system of poisons."

The side field was finished by one o'clock in the afternoon and yielded nothing; the metal detector gave no tug or pull to signal a companion metal in the earth. Leo and Gussie took turns consoling their prisoner in the parlor. Following lunch, Andrew took a stroll down Thale Road and was gratified by what he found but said nothing of what he'd seen; that had to come later, but he felt almost shy about it. At three o'clock a state police car drew up to the house and two officers brought out Mr. Gravino-Griggs in handcuffs but this Andrew didn't see, for he had been running the metal detector down the path to the pond, where he stole a brief swim to cool off. Tarragon reported to him later that both Gussie and Leo had followed the police to the car, explaining to them— or trying to—that Mr. Griggs was a very fine actor and well known to them, but had been too poor to resist bad company.

"Ask Artemus" were Leo's final words to them. "Tell them he's Hamlet, damn it, he'll remember."

But Artemus, of course, was delivering the mail on his afternoon rounds.

The rows between the vegetables were walked through with the detector, and the ground between the house and the road were swept. Hot, tired and exhausted they at last gave up their search and at six o'clock returned to the kitchen, where Tarragon made cucumber and tomato sandwiches for them. But no one touched their supper.

"We've covered every inch," Gussie said in a discouraged voice. "Except for the woods, but I cannot imagine—"

"We can't try the woods," Leo said firmly. "Absolutely not, she'd never have buried anything in the woods."

"She could have—if she'd left a map," pointed out Gussie, and with a sigh, "We have to give up, have to." To Andrew she said, "Mr. Margus was going to send a cable to your father about his not owning the land now. We'll just have to accept Mr. Margus's suggestion and sell the woods. You think your father would be interested in buying twenty-two or twenty-three acres?"

Andrew thought his father would be far more interested in berating him for ever finding Harriet Thale's will. He said truthfully, "I wouldn't count on it, but Mr. Crumbull of *Bear and Crumbull* seemed eager."

The moment had come for him to make his statement, and he nervously cleared his throat. "In the meantime I have something to say to you that you must all hear."

He was looked at with surprise.

"Yesterday," he told them, "when my mother and I took the bus into Pittsville we didn't just rent the metal detector, we also visited the electric company."

"Electric company?" said Gussie blankly.

He nodded. "To ask the cost of reconnecting your house with electricity, which—considering what I still have in my savings account in the bank—is affordable for me. And this afternoon, as promised, there were two men down on Thale Road checking the lines, and also the poles for termites."

"Lines? Poles?" said Miss L'Hommedieu, frowning. "Termites?"

"Oh," gasped Tarragon. "Oh Andrew!"

"It may take as long as a week," he explained, "but you'll have electricity very soon for the winter—and the oil tank filled, too—for at least one year, which should give you time to—well, find the right buyer for the land if it's necessary, seeing how there's no money."

Gussie had heard him out and now said fiercely, "We don't take charity, Andrew, you hear me? We do not accept charity."

On stronger ground now, Andrew smiled. "But it's not charity, Gussie, it's a bribe. Actually it's blackmail."

"Blackmail!" exclaimed Gussie.

"Yes, because you'll have to take me along with the electricity. I want to stay here with you for that one year, Gussie. I may never write another book again but I'm growing more and more cheerful by the day. It's good for me here."

"Hot baths," murmured Miss L'Hommedieu.

"No outhouse," said Leo in a startled voice. "Or pouring water into the tank of the toilet to flush it."

"Well, Andrew," said Miss L'Hommedieu, looking pleased.

"And we also get Andrew," pointed out Tarragon, beaming at him.

"Yes, me," he said, grinning back at her. "Well, Gussie?"

Gussie turned her back on them. "Leo," she said gruffly, "you haven't lighted the stove, we've no tea for our sandwiches, and here we are, all sitting around like bumps on a log. As for you, Andrew—" She stopped, and when she turned to him he saw there were tears in her eyes. "As for you, Andrew," she said, "we need four tomatoes for breakfast juice, and—and bless you, Andrew."

Immediately she brought out a loaf of bread from the drawer and began feverishly slicing it.

Andrew made a hasty retreat before he burdened them with any more gratitude, and closing the screen door behind him he headed for the tomatoes, quite aware that tomatoes were needed no more than the bread that Gussie was slicing.

Tarragon, following him, said, "Andrew, can you afford such—such generosity?"

"It's not generous," he told her firmly. "I can live here much more cheaply than in Manhattan, you wouldn't believe the rent on a studio apartment. And there'll be a job for me somewhere in Pittsville, it's an investment, that's all."

She leaned over and impulsively kissed him on the cheek. "Thank you," she said, and without thinking, Andrew's arms went around her. Refusing her cheek, his lips fastened on hers, and he kissed her so soundly that when they drew apart both of them were flushed and breathless.

"Oh!" she gasped.

"Should I apologize?"

"Don't you dare!" she told him.

"But I've only known you six days," he said. "You're young—and inexperienced, damn it. With men, surely?"

"You've just given me an experience," she pointed out. "You kissed me. I *liked* it."

"Yes, but according to my mother—what I mean is," he found himself stammering, "if anyone should fall in love with you they'd not want to take advantage—"

"For heaven's sake pick your tomatoes," she said indignantly. "You sound like someone out of a Victorian novel, Andrew."

"I *feel* like one, damn it," he shot back at her. "I can assure you it's new for me, but I have the most ridiculous interest in doing what's *honorable*."

"By calling me inexperienced? Insulting me? as if I'm a child? How *quaint*," she said scornfully, and stalked angrily back to the house.

He stared after her, feeling a fool and yet furious that she couldn't understand how many girls he'd kissed without the slightest desire to be protective or—well, honorable. He supposed he ought to explain, except that he was sure that he'd bungle this, too. He turned and saw that his mother was standing at the edge of the path, looking amused.

Strolling toward him she said, "You don't seem to have the savoir faire I expected, Andrew. Your first quarrel?"

"Not a quarrel," he said stiffly.

She linked her arm in his. "You've told them? about the electricity?"

He nodded. "Yes, and we've swept the entire area here with the metal detector today and found *nothing*, nothing at all."

His mother sighed. "A pity. Harriet would turn over in her grave if she knew. Obviously the letter was lost somehow, telling them where she buried her money."

"But to *bury* it?"

"I know, I know," she said, frowning. "But you have to understand that she sheltered so many people at different times that I daresay she preferred not to leave valuables in any obvious place in the house. She never cared if they were honest or not but it could have been a temptation to someone, which she would have understood and forgiven, but then she, too, would have been poor."

"There are such things as banks," he pointed out grimly.

"Yes, and some of it *was* in the bank, enough for the

expenses of running the house—your father inherited that, too. But she grew up in the Depression, Andrew. Banks failed, and besides," she added with a smile, "she was a Romantic, and part of her never ceased being a gypsy."

"And gypsies bury money?"

"Bury it or wear it sewed in their clothes—gold coins, of course, because they're portable, easily smuggled between countries and over borders, and certainly they lived precarious lives for centuries, not to mention the nearly million of them in Europe the Nazis shipped off to concentration camps to die. But I bear news, Andrew, I hear from Artemus that you had a great deal of excitement today?"

"And yesterday, but what's the news?"

"Artemus heard it within the hour, told Manuel, and Linda came running to tell me. The police have arrested Calvin Merkle in Pittsville, and they hope to arrest the others soon. It happened two hours ago."

"Well, they did their best to kill our burglar, so I'm glad for *him*."

Pausing at the porch, she said, "Not coming in?"

"I'm to pick four tomatoes. Told them about our visit to the power company and I'm afraid they'll keep thanking me."

"And your father?" she asked. "Has anything been heard yet from him? I assume he knows by now that he no longer owns Thale's Folly and never did."

Andrew felt a familiar tightening of unease. He said with feeling, "I really dread his reaction. When any cars arrive here—and traffic's been heavy today—I expect it to be him. Of course he'll be furious."

She smiled, and he thought how healthy and competent she looked, standing at the door. "I may have to come out of the closet," she said lightly. "Make an appearance to remind him about blood pressure, ulcers, and hypertension." She thought about it, shrugged, and went inside, leaving Andrew to sit among the tomato plants contemplating the various events of the day—but mostly Tarragon—and to pick four tomatoes.

Late that night Miss L'Hommedieu walked into Andrew's room to accost him. "Well, Andrew?" she demanded, "why are you doing this for us?"

He would have preferred to be flippant, to point out that since he was going to join them at Thale's Folly for a year he preferred hot water, an indoor bathroom and central heating, but while this would have neatly concealed his tenderer feelings it would only insult her.

He said honestly, "Because I can learn more living with all of you for a year than I could possibly learn in New York. Because you all make me feel part of a family . . . because I've discovered a mother again, living just across the pond. And because—" He hesitated.

"Because?" she said sharply.

He said ruefully, "Because there is one unalterable and indisputable fact that I've been learning all week: I love Tarragon."

Abruptly he sat down on the edge of his bed, burdened by the need to find words. "But I don't trust myself yet," he said, looking up at her. "I've lost my book writing, I've lost my job at Meredith Machines—"

Surrendering at last to flippancy, he added, "But it would be a hell of a long trip every weekend from New York to see her . . . the traffic's murder on weekends."

"Ah," murmured Miss L'Hommedieu, nodding, and with regal grace, looking satisfied and very pleased, she left him, closing the door behind her.

Saturday

11

[Basil,] being applied to the place bitten by venemous beasts, . . . it speedily draws the poison to it; *Every like draws its like* . . . Hilarius, a French physician, affirms upon his own knowledge, that an acquaintance of his, by common smelling to it, had a scorpion breed in his brain.
—Nicholas Culpeper, *The Complete Herball*, 1616

When Andrew came downstairs Tarragon was alone in the kitchen, seated quietly at the long table with her hands folded and her face thoughtful. Glancing up she said, "There was a—a sort of conference last night while you were out looking for Mr. Branowski."

He said quickly, "I didn't find him."

She nodded. "Nobody has found him. The conference was not exactly a happy one," she said. "They've decided to fully accept the fact there'll be no money to keep the woods and the pond." She added politely, "You've made it easier for them to accept this, Andrew, and they'd like you to know this . . . that at least they'll be comfortable now, with heat and light."

"But comfort," he said, "is small comfort for the loss of the woods and the pond." He sat down across the table from her. "No wonder you look sad," and considerably humbled he said, "Look here, I need to say I'm sorry, Tarragon, about what I so clumsily said yesterday. It isn't true, either, because you have experience in the one thing I know least about. And the most important."

She frowned. "What's that?"

"Love," he said. "You live with it, whereas I grew up full of anger and resentment and missed that." He reached out his hand. "Friends again?"

"Of course," she said, "but you do seem inarticulate at times."

"I write better than I talk," he told her. "It's *why* I write . . . or used to."

She laughed and reached across the table and grasped his hand, and then, "Tea," she said, releasing it and jumping up.

"Chamomile?"

"No, Saint John's Wort. It was an ancient belief that Saint John's Wort was so obnoxious to evil spirits that a whiff of it would cause them to fly away."

"We have evil spirits?" he quipped.

She didn't smile. "There's more," she said. "Your mother's just left, she came to tell me that *everyone's* worried now about Mr. Branowski. On his mail deliveries Artemus has been asking everyone if they've seen him, and he seems to have just disappeared. Your mother came to say that Manuel's wife Linda is going to begin calling hospitals this morning."

Andrew frowned. "But his knapsack still hangs from his tree?"

She nodded. "Untouched."

"You said he drinks," he pointed out.

"He's what Manuel calls a binge drinker. Remarkably sober for weeks and then a binge, but always in Tottsville, where people can find him. Yet nobody's seen him, drunk or sober, since Wednesday. He could have been hit by a car, or have had a heart attack and be lying somewhere in the woods."

"But you've searched the woods," he said.

"Every day, but there are other woods." She sighed. "He's such a dear old man, even the summer children are fond of him. Manuel *swears* he chose the kind of life he lives, just got fed up and took to the road."

"Where does he go when he leaves Tottsville?"

"He always leaves the first of September, like clockwork. We think he heads to Georgia for the winter. Linda likes to think he has a son or daughter there, or grandchildren, or someone. But no one *knows*."

Andrew said, "I was going to take the metal detector back to Pittsville this morning, but if I can help—"

"You might as well go, you don't even know what he looks like, except from the rear," she reminded him. "Manuel's garage is closed on Saturdays—"

"I know," he said with a smile, "I arrived on a Saturday." *Only a week ago,* he thought, and shook his head at how preposterous that felt now.

"—and he's rounding up some eager teenagers to search. Tottsville has two other ponds back in the woods where the summer people live. And lots of woods."

"Then I won't volunteer," he admitted. "Especially since

there's a bank in Pittsville that's open for three hours on Saturday and I need to cash a check. Need anything from town?"

"Only Mr. Branowski," she said ruefully.

With a glance at his watch, "I'll have breakfast in town. If I hurry I can catch the seven forty-five bus and be back to help later." He resisted a longing to kiss her good-bye; the electricity between them when he'd kissed her yesterday had been exhilarating but unnerving in its intensity.

On his way down the path Andrew stopped a minute to check Mr. Branowski's knapsack and bedroll, but nothing had been added or removed. After reaching the pond he took the shortcut to the highway, carrying the metal detector first in one hand and then the other; he was relieved when he could place it beside him on the bus.

Pittsville was a pleasant town, with elm-shaded streets and a town square with a lofty monument occupying its center. He returned the metal detector, produced enough identification to cash his check at the bank, and found Dina's Boutique just off the square, amused to see that one of his mother's very handsome sweaters was still displayed in its window. She had told him that Dina was in need of an assistant, preferably a man, and although he didn't go in, he could see Dina through the window: a plump, comfortable-looking woman with bright red hair. She looked easy to work with . . . a possibility, but nevertheless he bought a Pittsville newspaper for its want ads before climbing on the bus again.

Miss L'Hommedieu was seated in her usual chair on the porch when he returned. "Well, Andrew," she said kindly, "you missed the morning mail delivery. We received a card notifying us that our electricity is to be restored late Tuesday afternoon."

"Great! No termites, then. Do we run a contest for who gets the first bath?"

She bowed graciously. "We believe that you should have that honor, since it is your gift to us."

He bowed in turn. "I defer to you, Miss L'Hommedieu."

"I confess it will be exciting," she admitted. "Almost as exciting as the arrival of the Stephanovitches."

Startled, he said, "The who?"

"The gypsies. They should be here soon for two or three nights."

"From where?" he asked. "And where do they go?"

"They head north," said Miss L'Hommedieu, "and who knows where they come from in July, but in the winter Drushano and his brothers play music in restaurants. In New York City."

"Gorgeous music," said Tarragon eagerly, walking out of the kitchen. "Gypsy music—Rumanian—wait till you hear it! And during the winter Zilka and Tekla and the other women collect clothes, fascinating old clothes and jewelry—vintage stuff—for the summer, when they travel. They take booths at state fairs, or rent space at big flea markets to sell what they've collected, but every year in late July they start north for a big reunion with other members of the family on August first. New York state's just over the mountains"—Tarragon nodded westward—"and they meet at a campground somewhere in northern New York state where the owners are friendly . . . not being welcome everywhere," she added.

"Because they're gypsies?" said Andrew.

"Only when people realize they're gypsies. That's how Miss Thale met them . . . tell him, Miss L'Hommedieu."

Miss L'Hommedieu graciously obliged. "The police in Pittsville—this was many years ago—arrested them for camping south of the town. When Harriet heard of this she was *most* indignant, drove at once to the police station, where she interviewed the Stephanovitches, and then told the police they must come here to pitch on *her* land."

"Pitch tents?"

Tarragon laughed. "*Pitch* is just a word. Now they come in motor homes—four last year—and even have cordless telephones in them. And no, they don't steal," she said, seeing Andrew's face. "Why should they? You'll see!"

"Gold coins?" he said dryly.

"Lots. Earrings, necklaces . . ."

Miss L'Hommedieu smiled her ironic smile. "*Most* interesting people. Gadjakani once confided to me that in the early thirties, when the government ordered all *American* gold coins and bullion to be turned in for dollars—*paper* money to them—his father simply found a way to trade their American coins for *Mexican* gold pesos. One must," she said meditatively, "admire such ingenuity."

"I think they're going to interest me very much, especially since one of them witnessed my aunt's will," Andrew said, smiling. "And any sign of Mr. Branowski yet?"

She shook her head. "Your mother and Linda and I combed these woods all morning, even Bald Hill. We're going to let the others deal with the woods across the road now. I came back to go fishing so we can have trout tonight. Care to come?"

"Love to," he said.

"There's a sandwich for you in the kitchen," she told him. "I'll dig some worms while you have lunch." And picking up a bucket and trowel, she was gone.

Miss L'Hommedieu's story that evening seemed to match the ominous sounds of thunder and the flashes of lightning as a storm violently cooled and cleared the heat of the day.

" 'I dreamed that night of Elizabeth,' " she began, " 'and she was laughing. She had just stepped off the stage, it was the night they were performing *Lady Windermere's Fan*, and as she made her exit a shadow dimmed her face, her laughter dying, and she reached out her arms to me, but I was helpless. She looked at me with terror, as if she knew she was about to die—and then I woke, shivering.' "

There was an unhappy silence and then, "I hope," said Gussie in her practical voice, "that wherever Mr. Branowski may be, he has a roof over his head tonight."

Sunday

12

The root [of the Comfrey] boiled in water or wine and the
decoction drank, heals inward hurts, bruises, wounds and
ulcers. . . . The roots being outwardly applied cure; fresh
wounds or cuts immediately . . . for broken bones, so
powerful . . . to . . . knit together . . . it will join them
together again.

—Nicholas Culpeper, *The Complete Herball*, 1616

After helping Leo pick huge leaves of comfrey in the
morning, to be tied in clusters and hung to dry from
the parlor ceiling, Andrew chose a book to read from Leo's
well-stocked bookshelves and removed himself to the shade
of the tree on which the birds perched to wake him each day.
All of Leo's books were old and well thumbed. Andrew, avoiding those on unions, labor, politics, and philosophy, had
brought with him Christopher Morley's *Parnassus on Wheels*,
which he soon found delightful in spite of being unaccustomed to reading novels written eighty years ago. Presently,
sensing movement in a landscape empty of human beings, he
glanced up to see his mother emerging from the path carrying
a basket.

"I've come with four eggs to swap for mint from the garden," she told him.

"Any news on Mr. Branowski? You said Linda was going to try the hospitals."

"She did. No Mr. Branowski. And Artemus has checked out all the summer people but one: new people, renters with a house in Pittsville that caught fire, so they've decamped to deal with the damage, but they'll be back."

They walked together toward the house, his mother giving him a few quick furtive glances that led him to ask what was wrong.

She smiled. "Just admiring you, Andrew. You've already acquired a tan, and you've surely lost a few pounds—"

"On what we eat, that's no surprise."

"And you look healthy and fit, not at all the pale and bored young man I glimpsed when you first came. I'm *so* glad you're staying."

He said reluctantly, "I hate to leave but at some point this week I'll have to go back to Manhattan to close up my apartment and pack up my clothes, books, typewriter, and computer."

"How long?"

He shrugged. "Two days probably."

She nodded. "Rent a small van. Now who is *that*?" she asked as a sleek blue car lurched its way up the drive. "A gas guzzler," she announced disapprovingly. "Expecting someone?"

He shook his head, and then, "Oh my God, it's Father."

"It can't be!"

Andrew nodded. "He's heard about the will and he's furious."

His mother said calmly, "I've not seen him for seven years,

Andrew, I think I'll just shelter myself on the porch next to Miss L'Hommedieu's chair and wait—eavesdrop—to do battle for you if it's needed."

Andrew gave her an appreciative glance, and left to continue toward the driveway.

His father stepped out of the car, and Andrew realized he was driving his own car today. He stood beside it, watching Andrew's approach and frowning. "Andrew?" he said, as if not quite certain who he was.

"Who else?" said Andrew with a smile, and approaching him added bravely, "I suppose you've heard now from the lawyer."

"Heard?" he said. "Lawyer?"

"About the will that's been found."

"Will," he repeated. The glance that had been fixed upon Andrew drifted toward the woods, shifted to the sky, and returned to Andrew. "Is this Thale's Folly?"

Puzzled, Andrew said, "Thale's Folly, yes."

"I thought—I didn't know." His father's gaze moved with curiosity to the house and to the porch, where Andrew's mother stood in the shadows, and seeing her his frown deepened. "Allison?" he faltered. "*Allison?*"

"Hello, Horace," she said, moving out of shadow into the sunlight.

He took a step toward her and stopped. "Allison *here?*"

"Andrew, something's wrong," his mother said quietly. "Go to him."

Andrew stepped up to his father and touched his arm. "What's happened? Are you all right? What's happened?"

His father stared at him blankly.

Thoroughly alarmed now Andrew said, "Father, what's *happened*?"

"The most—most extraordinary thing."

"Yes, but what, Father?"

"The most—most extraordinary thing," he repeated. "I don't—don't really know why I'm here," he said helplessly. "I just got into my car to drive somewhere—anywhere." He shivered. "They don't want me anymore," he said. "After all these years, all I've done for them."

"Meredith Machines?" Andrew said incredulously. "They don't *want* you?"

"The merger—no room for me now. I'm fired."

"Surely you mean demoted?"

He shook his head. "Fired."

Quickly his mother crossed the driveway and glanced into the car. "The keys are inside, Andrew. Get your father into it at once, I'm driving him home. *Now.*"

"You mean to Bide-A-Wee?"

"For a cup of very strong nonherbal tea," she said impatiently. "It's for moments like this that God invented tea, preferably laced with brandy. Get him *in* the car, Andrew, Heaven only knows how he got here, he's in shock."

"I ought to go with you," he told her.

Seated at the wheel she turned her head to look at him. "Andrew, you're a dear, but this is strictly between your father and me." And to Horace, seated passively beside her now in the passenger seat, she said companionably, "You're not going to cry, are you, Horace?"

"Of course not," he snapped.

"Good," she said, and Andrew saw the twinkle in her eye as she gave him a glance that was positively roguish. "You see?" she told him. "He'll soon be himself again."

Backing the car out of the driveway at a reckless speed, she drove away down Thale Road.

With his father . . . Just like that—his *father*.

"So the mighty have fallen" was Leo's comment.

"Leo, you're being impertinent," said Miss L'Hommedieu. "You're speaking of Andrew's father, and the man who was Allison's husband. Have you no cup of kindness?"

"No need to quote 'Auld Lang Syne,' " growled Leo. "Sorry, Andrew. Just remembering good old Aeschylus, and his 'God, whose law it is that he who learns must suffer.' Apologies."

Andrew said dazedly, "I feel so shaken up; I never thought, never dreamed, it could happen to him. He looked so vulnerable, and ten years older. I mean, he was really a big man at Meredith. All those years—and twelve hours a day working on that merger!"

"Too many CEOs," Leo said, nodding. "You merge and you've got a hell of a lot of CEOs."

Miss L'Hommedieu said crisply, "I hope that you realize he had no idea your mother was here, Andrew, and came to find *you* in what is called his hour of need. Keep that in mind."

"He did, didn't he," he said in surprise. "Even though he wasn't sure where he was. But what on earth will he *do* now, he'll be lost."

Gussie smiled at him. "I suspect that your mother will decide that for him . . . Very competent woman, your mother."

A smile appeared on Andrew's face, and broadened into a grin as he considered this. "*That* will be a surprise for him . . . And he must have enough money to retire, except he's too young for it."

"Money," growled Leo. "Hubris!"

Gussie gave Andrew a shy smile. "And we shall do very nicely without your great-aunt's money, now that we've all agreed to sell twenty-three acres. We want you to know that, Andrew. I admit that I'm not partial to Swiss chalets—"

Tarragon interrupted to say eagerly, "But it needn't be Swiss chalets, Gussie, *you* own the property now, you can sell the land acre by acre, or to a developer who won't cut down all the trees or try to squeeze one hundred cottages into twenty-three acres like sardines in a can. You'll have time now for that, you quoted Mr. Margus as saying the legal business moves slowly. Probate and all. It's *you* who have control now."

"Control," repeated Gussie, looking pleased. "Me! How astonishing, let's find a new realtor tomorrow."

With a glance at Andrew, Tarragon said, "You still look in shock, Andrew, how about a swim?"

A change of scene at this point seemed very welcome. "Gladly," he said, and went in search of his swimsuit.

"Are you okay yet?" she asked as they walked in Indian file down the path to the pond.

He said ruefully, "No, I'm not, I've lost my anger."

"At your father," she said, nodding.

"Yes, and I don't know whether I feel pounds lighter, or—or cheated."

She turned and smiled at him. "You mean the emperor had no clothes on, and you never guessed."

"It needs adjustment," he admitted.

"Anger must be heavy to carry."

He laughed. "It's also a great stimulant. Let's swim!"

She dropped her towel on the beach and plunged into the water but Andrew stopped for a moment to look across the pond at the Bide-A-Wee cottage and wonder what was happening between his mother and father. He thought how strange it was that Thale's Folly had been slowly drawing all three of them together, as if by a magnet, when eight days ago he'd not even known of its existence.

The pond was already half-shadowed by gathering clouds; they swam contentedly, diving and splashing until at last they climbed out of the water to wrap themselves in towels and sit on Harriet Thale's boulder. Shivering, Andrew pointed off to his left, where the trees had thinned and a stripe of sunny green moss ran down to a cluster of rocks that edged the shore. He said, "Every time I've gone swimming I've thought what a perfect place for a house that would be. Just one room and loft to start with, and a balcony for the sun, and to be near the birds in that huge oak tree."

"Already planning to move out on us," she teased.

He turned and looked at her. "Only if I could take you with me."

He had startled her—himself as well—and she was silent, staring out at the pond that was slowly losing its glitter as the sky turned gray. After a long moment she turned and looked at him with her clear, honest gaze.

"I will tell you how it is with me, Andrew," she said softly. "I think you're wonderful, I really do, and I care. The minute I met you it was like magic—and I don't mean like Gussie's magic," she added with a smile, "but I felt I'd known you forever and ever, and I knew, just *knew*, we were going to be friends."

"Only friends?"

She leaned down from the rock, plucked a long blade of grass that had thrust its way into the light and said carefully, "You've felt really lost without the writing that's meant so much to you, Andrew. It's been your life, hasn't it? And as Leo likes to say, 'Nature abhors a vacuum.' "

He said in astonishment, "You think I regard you as just someone to fill a vacuum?"

"I don't know," she said gravely. "Do *you*? But I do know that I can't take the place of your writing, I refuse to be a substitute."

This silenced him for a moment. He knew that for every happy moment he'd experienced at Thale's Folly he'd been aware of its being shadowed by a waiting darkness, the knowledge that something precious had been lost. He said, "You mean you can't trust how I feel about you."

"Not until—" She hesitated.

"Until what?" he asked. "Until I'm full of lint like some damn vacuum cleaner?"

She laughed. "No, silly, but not writing anymore is your *real* nightmare. It's like an open wound, it really is, do you think we don't all of us see that, especially when Miss L'Hommedieu reads her stories every night? And that's how it will be, Andrew, until you either write again or stop feeling so lost without it. Anyway," she added, smiling, "you should feel grateful that I'm not snatching you up for a whirlwind summer romance, just to prove to Gussie that her incantations truly worked."

Frowning, he said, "Incantations?"

"Yes, that the first young man who came to our door would be the right one for me."

"*Wally Blore?*" he said in horror.

"Wally?" she said, laughing. "You're forgetting who came first, Andrew, it was you, not Wally."

"Good God," he said, and lightening the moment he clapped both hands to his head and said in mock dismay, "I give up, I give up, I'm outmaneuvered!"

"Good," she said, "because my teeth are chattering and I'm cold. Do let's go back to the house. As friends?"

"As friends," he conceded, but added warningly, "for another week, yes, but I can't promise more."

It rained hard that evening, and Miss L'Hommedieu was just finishing the end of her story, competing with the hard rain pelting the windows, when steps were heard outside on the porch. Miss L'Hommedieu paused, and they all turned in their chairs expectantly. Abruptly the door was flung open and a most astonishing woman stood on the threshold, eyes bright, lips smiling.

"And in all this rain!" cried Gussie. "You're wet!"

"Zilka," cried Tarragon, upsetting her chair as she rushed to hug her.

"We're in your meadow," Zilka said, and walking around the table she lightly touched Gussie on the shoulder, and then Leo, but when she came to Miss L'Hommedieu she gave her a long look, grasped her hand, lifted it to her lips and kissed it; almost, thought Andrew, as though a secret communication flowed between the two.

But what a strong face this woman Zilka had: a long nose, high cheekbones, full lips, a cleft in her chin, tangles of wet black hair only half concealed by the black kerchief she wore around her head. Whatever else she wore was hidden by a bulky trench coat—a man's, surely—and her face glistened with drops of rain.

"And who is this *gadjo*?" she asked, seeing Andrew.

"Allison's son," Gussie told her, "and Harriet Thale's nephew."

"Is he now!" she said, peering so closely at Andrew that he felt uneasy. "There is the likeness, you know—between him and our Drabani? And will he, too, travel under the good stars?" To Andrew, leaning even closer and smiling, "We call it *koosti cherino*, and may your stars be as good as hers."

"Do sit, Zilka," said Miss L'Hommedieu. "Have some tea."

"*Dordi*, but no. I come only to say tomorrow . . . *tomorrow* night the *patchiv*! In the morning we buy and kill chickens to cook over the fire for you all day, and in the night Chuka and Drushano and Michael will play their fiddles and we dance."

Leo grinned. "Last summer you bought your chickens at the grocery store, Zilka, you know you did."

She pinched his cheek affectionately. "You are a *beng*, Leo. You ate it, no?"

"But what if it rains?" asked Andrew, watching the glitter of her long gold earrings in the candlelight.

She swung on him in surprise. "But it will *not* rain," she said with authority. "I go." The door opened and she was gone, leaving behind only a pattern of raindrops on the floor.

Monday

13

[Betony] is good whether for the man's soul or for his body;
it shields him against visions and dreams, and the wort is
very wholesome.
                                                    —Apelius

With the promise of electricity on Tuesday, Andrew spent a few hours helping Leo carry up from the basement three floor lamps and seven table lamps. Having not yet experienced the cellar Andrew found himself fascinated by the similarity between it and Hobe Elkins's dump. There was, of course, the rescued space heater. There was the head of a mannequin, shelves of empty glass bottles and jars, a dozen lids of garbage pails, a tool bench, pipes, coils of wire, lampshades, and at least three dozen more books in a pile.

Looking around him with satisfaction Leo said, "This is *my* place."

Andrew nodded; he could conceive of no one else who would want it.

Since the lamps had reposed in the basement for nearly five years Gussie waited for them in the kitchen with dust cloths and broom, and they all had become involved in cleaning and admiring them when they heard the sound of a car on

Thale Road that grew loud enough to emphasize that it was not a lost tourist, but was heading up the driveway to Thale's Folly.

Going to the door they saw a huge and shining station wagon full of children making its way slowly up the driveway, bouncing over the rough spots. Fascinated, Gussie and Andrew walked out on the porch to see who it might be. It had no sooner stopped than a young woman in jeans and a T-shirt sprang out of the car, and seeing them shouted, "I'm so terribly sorry, I had no idea, I'm so *sorry*, I didn't *know*, I've only just heard and I'm so *sorry*."

"What is she sorry about?" asked Gussie. "Who is she?"

"What's up?" asked Andrew pleasantly, strolling toward the young woman, who appeared close to wringing her hands in apology.

"He's been with us all this time in Pittsville, helping us clear the—I'm Tippy Morton," she said. "We had this fire, and he's been such a help, and—"

"Who?" asked Andrew.

"*Who?*" asked Gussie.

Mrs. Morton turned with a flutter of hands toward the car. Among the tangle of children's heads in the rear there was motion, an adult head surfaced, a door opened, and a man stepped out.

"Mr. Branowski!" cried Gussie, and to Miss L'Hommedieu on the porch and to Leo and Tarragon in the kitchen, "It's *Mr. Branowski!*"

He looked pleased by his welcome, and Andrew, at once reaching for words to describe him, nodded. Hair still in damp strings—this he'd already seen before—but not the face, as brown and lined as old leather, with shaggy white eyebrows, a stubborn jaw, bad posture, a small shrunken mouth—no doubt lost teeth—and a twinkle in his eye as he looked them over.

Mrs. Morton was still trying to explain: Mr. Branowski had been hanging a swing from a tree for the children when the call had come about the fire at their house in town . . . Mr. Branowski was so handy, her husband a busy attorney, she'd asked Mr. Branowski to come and help—paying him, of course—and he'd been *such* a help carrying out charred beams . . . just one room, mercifully, the rest of the house barely singed, "but when I heard—" She stopped to catch her breath.

"It's all right," Gussie told her in hope of stopping her. "It's all right."

"I just didn't know, didn't *realize*—"

"It's *all right*," Andrew said in a louder voice, and walking up to Mr. Branowski said, "I'm Andrew Thale, how do you do, we've not met." And wondered what he might have been in his previous life, since he looked as dignified as a judge, even in filthy overalls and without teeth.

"We've missed you," Gussie told him.

"Needed you, too," said Tarragon. "Mr. Branowski, please come in and have tea, we've something to ask you."

"No, Tarragon," Gussie said. "Give it up."

"Chamomile?" asked Mr. Branowski.

Tarragon laughed. "Oh yes—at once!" and to Gussie, "We have to at least try, at least *ask*."

Six children emerged from the station wagon to say good-bye to Mr. Branowski, the two smallest ones hugging his knees. Mrs. Morton extracted bills from her purse, pressed them into his hand, and with a wave and shouts of good-bye, the station wagon backed down the drive and Mr. Branowski was ushered toward the house by Tarragon.

"Quite a welcome," he said with a chuckle, and to Miss L'Hommedieu, rising from her chair on the porch, he said, "And you, dear lady, how are *you*?"

"Tolerably well, Mr. Branowski, tolerably well."

"Leo?" called Gussie, opening the door to the basement. "We've found Mr. Branowski!"

Once Leo joined them they all sat down at the table, except for Tarragon, who busied herself brewing tea.

Leo said, "You start, Gussie."

"All right. It's about Harriet Thale, Mr. Branowski."

"Wonderful woman," he said, nodding. "Mind if I smoke?" He drew a cigarette butt out of a pocket; Leo at once handed him a match, and Tarragon, a saucer for the ash.

"We didn't know there was a will," Gussie told him. "Never found one, and the property went to her nearest relative, Andrew's father here," she said with a nod to Andrew.

His shaggy brows went up. "Never *found* the will!"

"Not until this week," said Leo.

"Through the most extraordinary circumstances," added Gussie.

Miss L'Hommedieu said dryly, "So extraordinary that we now find ourselves deeply indebted to a thief who tore apart Miss Thale's bedroom."

"It was behind the mirror," put in Andrew.

"And that's when we learned Gussie was left the property—and you witnessed the will, Mr. Branowski," added Tarragon. "You and Zilka Stephanovitch."

"That I did," he said, nodding.

"Fetch our copy of the will, Leo," said Gussie.

While they waited, Tarragon brought Mr. Branowski his cup of chamomile tea, added a spoonful of honey, and sat down.

Leo, returning, placed the will on the table for Mr. Branowski and said, "Read."

"Why?" he asked. "I remember what it says."

"Refresh your memory, it's been six years and we need help."

Mr. Branowski carefully read the will and put it down. "What help? I've read it, what is it you think I'd know that you don't?"

"Where she buried her gold," blurted out Andrew.

"Because," Tarragon said, "we're going to have to sell the woods and the pond and everything except the house to pay inheritance taxes and the lawyer, and—"

Andrew interrupted to say, "You've read the will, she said there'd be a letter, but there wasn't any letter. We've done our best, but burying means digging . . . and *twenty-five acres?*"

"We thought," Gussie said, "that you might remember something—just something—about where it was buried. Something she said."

Mr. Branowski looked at her blankly. "Why would she have said anything? It's not needed."

Gussie said patiently, "But there was no *letter*, Mr. Branowski, she *said* there was a letter but she left us with no clue at all."

"But it's right here," said Mr. Branowski. "Right in front of your eyes."

"What is?"

"You don't see it?" He held up the will to show them. "She didn't want it plainly said, not in front of Zilka. Miss Thale trusted Zilka, but she didn't trust Zilka's brother Bruno. Maybe if you'd seen this will five years ago you'd have been sharper. You didn't notice these last words here? See how she added, 'be wise about this, Tarragon' and underlined the words?"

It was their turn to stare at him blankly.

"She buried her money," he said, "and she added 'be wise about this, Tarragon.' Didn't you think it odd, those five words added at the end? There was no need for a letter."

"Why not?" gasped Gussie.

"Because," he said patiently, "it's buried in the garden under the tarragon."

"Under the—can this be true?" whispered Gussie.

A stunned Leo said, "We thought it meant for Tarragon to be wise about being left a lot of money, being so young."

"Can this be *real*?" Gussie said, grasping the will and staring at the words.

"The Lord works in mysterious ways," pointed out Miss L'Hommedieu.

"So did my great-aunt," Andrew said dryly.

Mr. Branowski gave him a sharp glance. "And you, young man, would *you* leave directions around where anybody might see, telling exactly where money's buried? But I'll say one thing: she thought you'd know. *'They'll know,'* she said."

"Except we didn't," said Leo.

He and Gussie exchanged glances; Miss L'Hommedieu looked at them expectantly; Andrew looked at Tarragon, and Mr. Branowski waited, twinkling, and then, "Let's *go!*" shouted Leo. "Where's the shovel?"

All of them except Miss L'Hommedieu jumped up from the table. "It's on the porch," said Miss L'Hommedieu, rising calmly to follow Mr. Branowski out of the door.

Leo reached the herb garden first, Andrew having stopped to pick up a pointed trowel abandoned among the kale. Once inside the encircling, rosemary-covered wall of rocks, Leo strode to the farthest end of the tarragon row, muttered, "Here goes," and placing one foot on the shovel he plunged it deep into the earth. They waited in suspense.

"There's *something* here," he said cautiously.

"Of course there is," said Mr. Branowski.

"But oh, the tarragon," mourned Miss L'Hommedieu. "Be careful, Leo."

Leo neatly turned the spade in the earth, prying up stalk and roots of tarragon to expose the corner of what looked to be a metal container. As he carefully freed it from the earth the edge of a second receptacle could be seen. Carefully, reverently, Leo lifted the first one out and deposited it on the earth. "Steel," he said. "Somebody open it!"

Gussie stepped forward and made an attempt to pry it open. "We need a screwdriver," she said, "or a knife."

"Let me try," Tarragon said, and recklessly attacking the

box with a rock she forced it open. Startled, she cried, "But these are just *papers*!"

Andrew, peering over her shoulder, smiled. "Those are *bonds*. A whole pile of them!"

"Oh Leo, see what the next box holds," Tarragon told him. "This is *exciting*."

The second box proved exciting indeed. It was long and narrow and very heavy, and snapped open as easily as the metal clip on a safe-deposit box. "Dear God in heaven!" gasped Gussie as Tarragon reached inside and drew out a handful of gold coins.

"All shapes and sizes!" she said in awe. "And *gold*. The box is *full* of them, aren't they beautiful?" She handed a coin to Miss L'Hommedieu and one to Gussie.

"Exquisite," whispered Miss L'Hommedieu.

"And one for you, too, Mr. Branowski," she said, beaming at him. "If not for you—!"

"Like pirate treasure," Leo said in an awed voice.

Andrew, intrigued by Leo's success—*what the hell*, he thought—decided to dig for pirate treasure at *his* end of the row, and inserting his trowel under the tarragon, delving deep below its roots, he called out, "Hey—I've hit something, too!" Without venturing any deeper he moved a few feet along the row and tested the earth again, then advanced slowly toward Leo at the far end, where he said in an astonished voice, "This entire row of tarragon has metal boxes buried under it!"

They turned to stare at him, and Gussie looked suddenly frightened. "Leo—no more! Stop! This is too *much*."

Miss L'Hommedieu nodded. "She's right, it's too much."

Mr. Branowski, lingering at a discreet distance, said, "Safest place to leave it, anyway. No need to worry about *me*, I knew where this was buried a whole year before Miss Thale died. Think I'd touch it now? I'd rather have my tree." He frowned. "Nobody's stolen my knapsack and tarp, have they?"

Andrew assured him that both knapsack and tarpaulin were still safely under his tree.

"So we stop?" asked Leo, resting on his shovel.

Andrew, considering this, said, "The question certainly does arise as to what you'd do with anything more that's dug up, my trowel must have hit at least five more metal containers. You'd need a car, a bank, a safe-deposit box, a dealer to appraise the coins or sell them, a stockbroker to handle the bonds—"

"Stop—stop, it's terrifying," Gussie said. "So *much*! I never *dreamed*—"

"I think," said Miss L'Hommedieu judiciously, "one might carry just this *one* box of coins to the house. To admire."

Gussie nodded, looking relieved. "What matters is knowing that it's here. And that we needn't sell the woods and the pond, and—and—" She burst into tears.

Leo sighed. " 'Care certainly clings to wealth' indeed, just as Horace wrote."

"But do carefully replant the tarragon you've uprooted," said Miss L'Hommedieu. "*Carefully*, Leo."

They now became busy planting the tarragon that had been dug up, which amused Andrew. If Gussie was in tears, and Tarragon comforting her, Andrew found that he had to conceal an insane urge to laugh, a laugh that began deep down inside of him and wanted to break out but dared not. Whether there was a hysterical aspect to it he had no idea, but he had never before observed a scene fraught with such conflict: such terror at the thought of riches, or such delight in finding them.

Most of all, he was absurdly happy for them. The woods would remain unviolated, the pond unpolluted, Gussie's shrine intact, the birds would continue to live, and sing, and build nests at Thale's Folly; there would be no Swiss chalets, Miss L'Hommedieu would have a hot bath every day for the rest of her life, and in the evening there was to be a *patchiv*.

14

If [Agrimony] be leyd under mann's heed,
He shal sleepyn as he were deed;
He shal never drede ne wakyn
Till fro under his heed it be takyn.

—Medieval English medical journal

Before any *patchivs*, barbecues, or Stephanovitches, Andrew knew in the morning that he could no longer contain his curiosity as to what was happening at Bide-A-Wee cottage. Apparently everyone else was sleeping late after the excitement of the day before; the decoding of the will by Mr. Branowski, he thought, was surely an accomplishment as staggering as the translation of the Rosetta stone. He tiptoed downstairs, spread blueberry jam on a slice of bread, scribbled a note reporting that he had gone to tell his mother the good news, and leaving it on the table set out for Bide-A-Wee. Zilka had said there would be no rain today, and there was no rain. Perhaps she, too, was a witch, he thought with a smile, but his smile died away as he reached the stepping-stones across the brook and approached the highway. Had his father recovered, he wondered; had he returned to New

York? Had he and his mother quarreled? He'd forgotten all the quarrels he'd overheard as a child, but he was remembering them now.

He was relieved to see his father's blue car parked at the edge of the highway, and with increasing suspense he walked up the graveled path to the cottage.

"Come in, the door's unlocked," his mother called out.

He opened the door. His mother and father were seated at the long table by the window with a carafe of coffee between them, and newspapers and sheets of paper nearly covering the table. His mother said cheerfully, "Bring a cup from the kitchen, Andrew, and join us for coffee."

"Good morning, Andrew," his father said, as formally as usual, and then, "Get the damned cup so we can get on with things here."

Andrew entered the tiny kitchen and returned with a cup decorated with elves, no doubt another flea-market acquisition. "On with what things? And I must say you're looking rested, Father," he said as his mother filled his cup with coffee.

His father ignored this. "Pull up a chair," he told him. "Now where were we, Allision?"

"Let's see, we've added up your pension," she said, "and the silver balloon you'll receive—or is it a parachute?—and we've crossed off—" She stopped and glanced at Andrew, smiling. "Your father and I have discussed his living here with me for a while. *Not* marrying," she added firmly. "So many of you young people live together without the banns there seems no reason why we can't."

"When we were married we quarreled," his father pointed out.

"Oh, we'll quarrel anyway," she assured him blithely. "Now where were we?"

"What *are* all those sheets of newspaper and paper?" asked Andrew.

"Possibilities," said his father. "I daresay we can use your input, Andrew."

This was amazing indeed. "Always glad to help," he said brightly. "What possibilities are you discussing?"

"We've discarded the idea of a bicycle repair shop," his mother told him, "but according to yesterday's *Gazette* there are several businesses for sale or going bankrupt."

His father frowned. "This newspaper for sale has its appeal, Allison. One of those 'freebies' full of ads the *Gazette* wants to rid themselves of."

"Yes, but you're not terribly good at selling ads, are you, Horace?" she asked tactfully. "Turn to page two, there's a rather sad article about a small plastics factory going out of business. Human-interest story. The owner's been in Pittsville for thirty-five years, he's going to have to close—no buyers—and fifteen workers will lose their jobs."

His father, turning to page two, frowned over it. "Makes dinnerware."

"Yes," she said, "I've seen it . . . quite dull. But if someone bought it, hired a very *good* designer—"

Here Andrew's glance moved with interest to the colorful skeins of wool in the corner.

"—someone who could design really exciting and outrageous colors and patterns, they might do very well in boutiques and the more avant-garde shops. What a challenge it would be," she said deliberately. "And you know plastics, don't you?"

Andrew moved from amazement to awe. Leo had been right, his mother would know precisely how to divert and rescue his father and she had the confidence and tact to do it. It also startled him to realize that quite possibly she still loved him. He said, "I hate to interrupt this conference—and you make awfully good coffee, Mother—but I've good news to tell. Mr. Branowski's been found, and Harriet Thale's money was buried under the tarragon."

She stared at him, wide-eyed. "Under the *tarragon!*" She frowned. "You mean—oh, why didn't *I* see that? Those words added at the end, was that it?"

Andrew nodded.

She shook her head. "And I thought it was advising Tarragon to be wise about inheriting money at a young age."

"So did Leo. You do know, Father, that the will's been found and you don't own Thale's Folly after all?"

His father brushed this aside casually. "So your mother told me at breakfast this morning."

"But only after he'd slept for ten hours," added his mother.

Andrew grinned at her. "Then I think I'll leave you both to your Machiavellian plottings. The Stephanovitches have arrived, and there's a *patchiv* tonight if you care to come."

"Too busy," said his father.

"Not necessarily," his mother added. "We'll see how it goes."

His father gave Andrew a stern look. "We'll also be looking into some travel . . . your mother's always wanted to see Alaska, but I've been too busy."

It was also possible, he realized, that his father still loved his mother. A speechless Andrew managed only a feeble "Yes," and then as he reached the door he rallied to say, "See you later."

But neither of them heard him, and in spite of being ignored he left with a broad smile on his face that turned into a chuckle, and then to an outright laugh as he made his way back to Thale's Folly.

The day proved full of Stephanovitches. Andrew's hand was shaken by men named Asani, Yorko, Michael, Luigi, Chuka, and Drushano; gypsy children splashed in the pond during the afternoon, and the cleared area next to the meadow was full of wood smoke. By sunset, the eight barbecued chickens had been dispatched, their bones claimed by Gussie for soup stock, and Tarragon escorted Miss L'Hommedieu back to the house, where she would most enjoy the music from her chair on the porch, she said. When Tarragon returned she had changed from her blue jeans into a long white skirt—"from my high school graduation," she told Andrew—and she had added the glittering black sequin jacket that he'd found for her at the thrift shop. "You look gorgeous," he told her, "and as a friend—" He leaned over and kissed her. "Strictly as a friend, of course."

"To that," she informed him, "I could very crassly say 'Oh

yeah?' " and with a smile crossed the meadow to help Zilka move chairs.

Drushano and his two brothers were tuning their violins on the steps of one of their mobile homes, and Andrew wandered over to observe them. Drushano, seeing him, smiled, and lifting his bow he played a few notes of music that startled Andrew.

He said, "My God, you make that violin sing! That's 'Boogie-Woogie Stomp,' isn't it?"

"Ah, you know boogie-woogie?"

Andrew nodded. "Jazz and boogie-woogie I collect. Where do you play in New York?"

He named a well-known restaurant in the Village, "and sometimes uptown," he said with a shrug.

Andrew would have talked more with him but the other two were waiting for Drushano, and he saw that neighbors had begun arriving, people acquainted from past summers with Miss Thale and her gypsies, and among them Artemus and Manuel with their wives. It had grown darker now, and as the moon rose in the east Zilka brought out four lanterns, lighted them, and hung them from the trees. Drushano and his brothers moved to a commanding position under a lantern, and Drushano spoke.

"'We play first the 'Horo—Hora Lui Dobrica,' folk music from a beloved Rumania."

Three violins were lifted, and with a flourish of bows the men began to play.

It was a perfect choice for a celebration, lilting and joyous, not music for social dancing; it needed a ballet with jubilant leaps to express its joy; it soared and swept, it was exhilarating and ended on a high exuberant note. But nothing prepared Andrew for what came next. Luigi, seated next to him, leaned over to whisper, "This will be *real* gypsy music, I will tell you the words."

The music began again, but in a low key, like a dirge, and Luigi murmured, "The winter snows are falling . . ." Andrew made no reply, he had turned mute and still as the sad notes reached and stirred him; he felt the poignancy, the melancholy, the emotion invoked by these stringed instruments, so masterfully played they fairly throbbed with pain, loneliness, and grief. From exhilaration Andrew was plunged into mourning, and tears came to his eyes. *The winter snows are falling . . .* It was suddenly unendurable, and in panic he stumbled to his feet and fled.

Into the woods he ran, faster and faster to escape the music that haunted him even now until, seeing light ahead—the flicker of a candle—he found himself at Gussie's altar and flung himself on the moss.

Gussie must have come here earlier and lighted the candle— to pray? to give thanks? He realized how deeply the music had stirred him—*too* deeply—breaking through a wall in him that opened him up to the darkness he'd tried to bury for so many months. Dimly, still, he could hear the music, or had he carried it with him?

The moss was like a soft carpet; he ran a hand over it tenderly, caressing it, bringing him back to this moment, and then he lifted his eyes to the altar, to the flickering candle, and, "Why?" he asked of Gussie's gods, the earth, moon, sun, and stars, and then, *"Why?"* he demanded aloud, as he'd done so many times, but there was no answer.

His thoughts drifted back in time to the Andrew he'd once been . . . inviolable, or so he'd believed, confident of his future, buoyed by early success, already sketching out possibilities for a new book, anticipating a larger advance, perhaps a larger Manhattan apartment, and then—in one nanosecond—all gone.

He realized he'd spent months damning the trick that life had played on him, damning his friend for piloting a plane that crashed, damning the terror that had strangled all interest in what he'd loved doing—and yes, consuming him with self-pity—and in a blaze of revelation he understood that Miss L'Hommedieu had been right after all.

He had been angry at God—and he'd not even known that he believed in God.

It was embarrassing to admit his arrogance: he had never asked why the engine of the plane had failed, to present him with the torment of an early death; what had angered him and stunned was that God had allowed it to happen to him.

To *him*, Andrew Thale.

It stunned him now, in *this* moment, to understand that all these months he'd been talking, not to himself, but to God.

Miss L'Hommedieu had known this. It was suddenly important—terribly important—to find and talk to Miss L'Hommedieu, whose prescience implied what . . . knowingness? madness? wisdom? At least an acquaintance with God. And with life.

He staggered to his feet and ran.

She was still seated in her chair on the porch, stationed there to hear the music in the woods, but he was surprised to see that Gussie was with her, standing beside her, one hand resting on Miss L'Hommedieu's shoulder. He thought he had left Gussie nodding happily at the Rumanian folk song in the woods, but now she was here, and with a strange look about her.

Andrew said with a smile, "I came back to talk with Miss L'Hommedieu."

"She's left us," said Gussie.

An idiotic thing to say, he thought, with Miss L'Hommedieu seated erect, eyes wide open, and wondered why he suddenly tensed.

The screen door opened and Leo walked out, followed by Mr. Branowski. "She's dead," he told Andrew, and to Gussie, "Let her go, Gussie. It's time we carry her upstairs to her bed before—" He stopped, unable to say it.

Gussie nodded, and withdrew her hand. Suddenly aware of Andrew she said, "Find Tarragon, will you? and your mother?" Her face grew stern. "But don't stop the music, don't stop the dancing, she always loved that."

Andrew stood very still, staggered by a wrenching sense of loss. He felt—and it was very strange to him—as if he'd been kicked in the heart. It was only when his eyes brimmed with tears that he turned away to retrace his steps and find Tarragon and his mother.

Later, when the house had quieted, Andrew ventured into Miss L'Hommedieu's room alone to see her.

She was lying on her bed, very white, calm and remote; Gussie had placed coins on her closed eyes, and the blue-feathered boa around her shoulders, and seeing the boa the tears returned to Andrew's eyes. He approached her shyly, half expecting her to open her eyes and say "Well, Andrew?" but her eyes remained closed.

"Miss L'Hommedieu," he said aloud. "Miss L'Hommedieu?"

There was, of course, no response.

He touched her hand; it was only a little cold, and kneeling beside her he grasped it firmly in his. "Miss L'Hommedieu," he said, "I have grown very fond of you and I think—I hope—you knew that. I only wish I had known you longer—and better."

He looked at the calm, lined face, so inscrutable now, and could think of nothing more to say until, "I want you to know, Miss L'Hommedieu," he said, "that you cast a very long shadow."

Tuesday

15

Above the lower plants it towers,
The Fennel with its yellow flowers;
And in an earlier age than ours
Was gifted with the wondrous powers
Lost vision to restore.

—Longfellow

No one slept that night. The gypsies had gone—"they're superstitious about death," Gussie told him—and although Miss L'Hommedieu had left them, too, a sense of her presence lingered to sweeten the sour taste of a party that had ended badly. "Only a few more hours," said Andrew sadly, "and she could have had a bath in that lovely mahogany tub."

Gussie said sharply, "She wouldn't want us to mourn her"—and rising from the breakfast table—"Tarragon, I want you to pick a bouquet for her. She was very partial to Queen Anne's lace, wasn't she?"

"And anything blue," said Tarragon, nodding.

"A *large* bouquet"—and turning to Andrew—"There's a small trunk in her room, she said she kept her poetry books in it. See if you can find a poem to read over her grave, will you?"

190

This was the least he could do for her, he thought as he mounted the stairs; he could certainly sift through a few books to find if any poem reflected an astringent and uncommon Miss L'Hommedieu. He would hope for a poem full of flowers and lace, of a woman with eyes as black as jet in a lined face. Wordsworth? Keats?

Her room held the scent of lavender. The trunk under the window was a small affair, shabby and old, and there was no key. What could he expect, he wondered, a few sentimental trophies from the past? For that matter, what *was* her past? He opened its lid reluctantly, feeling an intruder, but there looked to be only two old books, a collection of colorful feathers, bits of lace and ribbons, a small, very primitive wood carving of a man, a faded birthday card from someone named Rene, who had written, "My thoughts are always with you." There was no envelope. Andrew picked up the slender hardcover book, its cover red with gilt letters and with a drawing of African natives in one corner. "*Mission Work in Central Africa,*" he read, "by James Stevens Arnot, With an Introduction to the Bemba Language by the Author." Its copyright date was 1882.

An odd book to cherish, and certainly not poetry.

The second book had a plain blue paper cover, and its title was: *Report of the Commission of Inquiry, appointed to inquire into the Circumstances attending the murder of Basil Hopkins French, and the notorious trial that followed, with Record of Evidence taken, and other Documents.* Printed by the Government of Northern Rhodesia, 1947.

Northern Rhodesia? This was curious, he thought, and then—*Basil Hopkins French?*

"Basil Hopkins French!" he blurted out, startled by his own voice in the silent room.

Familiar, *very* familiar, but why?

Miss L'Hommedieu!

He ceased kneeling and abruptly sat down on the floor beside the trunk and opened the Commission of Inquiry. There was a table of contents listing a Diary of the Commission; Findings of the Commission, Part I, Part II, Part III; List of Exhibits, Names of Witnesses, Evidence Heard, Address to the Commission, Correspondence between the Government of . . .

Impatiently he turned to part I, entitled "The Circumstances Attending the Death of Basil Hopkins French & the Events Leading Up to It."

He read, "On the 10th of October, 1946, which is the last day on which French was seen alive, it is clear from the evidence of the natives that Basil Hopkins French left the Missionary Station that is administered by Miss Emily L'Hommedieu in midafternoon . . ."

Missionary Station? *Miss L'Hommedieu?* He realized that his mouth had dropped open . . . she of the flowing chiffon gowns and flowered hats? She had lived in *Africa?*

Ignoring detail he turned pages quickly until, "French was found lying on the ground on his left side and hidden by tall grasses, head thrown back, right arm extended at full length near the body with the palm of the hand upward and the left arm bent. There was blood on the head and hair, a hole or holes in the head, and one under the chin. According to Dr. Rene Roget, death had occurred four days earlier."

But who *was* Basil Hopkins French?

Thumbing through the pages he found an interminable number of natives who had been questioned in detail, identified as Chief Mwanta Kutemba, Christian, from Domo village; Sombo Luwej, pagan, Kitalo village; Kayomba Chibwa, Christian, of Domo village; Kayombu Chibwa, pagan, Kitalo village; with here and there an English name, of a District Officer, doctor, veterinarian . . . but he was not interested in who had found the body or when and how, or who went where or did what or knew what, he turned pages quickly, searching for explanations, answers, a conclusion. He found it in the last three pages in the official report, written by the Acting Governor to the Secretary of State for the Colonies in London, and marked CONFIDENTIAL.

"Sir," he read. "Referring to Sir Martin Smythe's confidential dispatch (No 3), transmitting a copy of the Commission of Inquiry into the case of the late Basil Hopkins French, I now have the honor to inform you that the Commission have concluded their investigations and have submitted their Report, two copies of which . . ."

Andrew skipped to the next paragraph.

"As regards the circumstances attending the murder of Mr. Basil Hopkins French, the finding of the Commission is inconclusive. I take this opportunity to record that all the investigations which have been made into this case, notwithstanding the notoriety of the trial that followed, have failed to disclose grounds upon which a criminal charge could have been laid against Miss Emily L'Hommedieu with any chance of success."

Criminal charge? Miss L'Hommedieu? *His* Miss L'Hommedieu?"

The report continued: "Turning to the conduct of the Native Authorities in this case, I have already reported to you that Chief Kutemba of Domo village was tried before a special magistrate, who was sent from the capital for the purpose, on a charge of conspiracy to obstruct the course of justice, and was sentenced to ten months imprisonment with hard labor. At the same time two other natives, Mbumba Ndale and Chibinda Toloshi, were convicted under the same sections and sentenced to terms of imprisonment of eight months and six months respectively. These convictions were quashed on appeal to the High Court."

Conspiracy! Another shock, and a dazed Andrew continued reading.

"It has proven impossible, from the material available, for any firm conclusion to be formed as to who was responsible for the murder of Basil Hopkins French. As noted (page 141, paragraph 3) the testimony of Dr. Rene Roget was vague almost to the point of being misleading, but according to the District Officer and three natives, his alibi proved unimpeachable.

"You will note (page 13, Part I) that Miss L'Hommedieu had met the deceased in America, that he had arrived six months previous to his death to persuade her to marry him, and the only statement given by Miss L'Hommedieu to the District Officer was that 'Africa changed him.' Following this she disappeared and her whereabouts remain unknown despite every effort to find her."

Another shock . . . disappeared?

"It may be taken as established that Basil Hopkins French was abusive to the natives," continued the report, "and according to Dr. Rene Roget's testimony, he was seen to strike Miss L'Hommedieu on one occasion. It is known that Miss L'Hommedieu had not been popular with her superiors at the mission station in the capital, insisting the magic practiced by the witch doctors—not witches, she emphasized, but witch doctors—appeared to be more successful than either her prayers or the pills she dispensed, and that she counted Chief Kutemba 'a very good friend.' On the other hand, Mr. French referred to natives as animals, kaffirs, or swine.

"We can only regret," concluded the report, "the unfortunate attention accorded this trial in the newspapers of Africa and Europe, and express the sincere hope that any relatives of Basil Hopkins French may find consolation in the fact that every attempt was made to unearth the truth, but that this Government, in its finality, is prepared to accept the tribunal's conclusion of murder by person or persons unknown."

Not person, thought Andrew, *but persons.*

He sat back on his heels in astonishment, trying to connect this with the Miss L'Hommedieu he knew. Africa! . . . Northern Rhodesia was Zambia now, wasn't it? and in 1946 it would have been a British protectorate, or some such, and she had *lived* there? She would have been young—it was fifty years ago, after all—and she would probably have worn a cork hat—that was de rigueur in those days, wasn't it? Her face would have been unlined, and perhaps her hair had been as black as her jet eyes. He pictured her as eager and idealistic; perceptive, too, he thought, this much was obvious from her appreciation of the natives' culture, when in those days they'd no doubt have been considered savages.

What could have happened on that day or night when Basil Hopkins French had been murdered? The report hinted at conspiracy; had Miss L'Hommedieu known that her errant lover was going to be murdered? The chief of the village had been a "good friend" to her. Had she been part of the conspiracy, if there was one? What had she felt when Basil Hopkins French was found murdered: relief? guilt? grief? And her strange disappearance, did it suggest help from persons wanting to protect her, or to prevent her from testifying?

He would read the inquiry in detail—all 149 pages of it, and then—yes, he would even read the book on missionary life, with its introduction to the language of Bemba, which she must have learned and spoken.

He realized that he had never considered anyone's past but his own—had nearly drowned in his, as a matter of fact. The mystery of this captured him.

My God, he thought, *she could have killed him, and if not, she must have known who did.* He wondered if she had been dismissed in disgrace by his missionary society; he wondered what nuances had made the trial so notorious; he wondered what her relationship had been with Dr. Rene Roget, in whose thoughts she had remained; he wondered what had happened to her in all the years since that long-ago murder trial.

She had said to him, "Once, long ago, I met with Reality

and found it so pitiless and chilling that I have taken great pains to avoid it ever since." He remembered, too, the evening when he'd talked of murder as he sketched her portrait. "And have you ever met a murderer?" she had inquired tartly. "Even a sophisticated one?"

He rose and went to the window and looked down into the garden below, with its neat rows of green beans and broccoli, and saw that Miss L'Hommedieu's garden chair was still in place waiting for her.

She would miss the August harvest.

And he would miss *her*.

He thought that if spirits lingered for a time after death, and she was in this room with him now, at this moment, she must be very amused at his discovery, and not at all disconcerted. "Well, Andrew?" she would say with that faint, ironic smile.

He thought, *She has brought curiosity—yes, and a sense of wonder—into my life.*

The astonishment of her!

She deserved more than a poem. He turned and walked out of her room and into his own, and drawing notebook and pen from his knapsack he placed them on the table. He sat back a moment, thinking and remembering, but the words returned to him with a surprising clarity, and surely she'd not mind his borrowing them, at least for this moment.

"Well, Miss L'Hommedieu?" he said challengingly, and on this hot and breezeless day he felt a sudden draft of cold air across his back; the curtains at the window fluttered and then stilled.

With a nod he picked up his pen and began to write: "The fires were burning late that night, small coins of brightness against the impenetrable dark. There were no drums, for the night could be full of ears and what they planned must never be heard . . . Calmly, gravely, they discussed death.

"The death of Basil Hopkins French."

He paused. There would be weeks of research ahead, a good Bemba dictionary to find, letters to write to Zambia and to London, documents and old news clippings to collect, Dr. Roget to trace, and every word of evidence studied in those 149 pages—*wonderful*, he thought—and with a rush of excitement he entered that African night to begin steeping himself in the mystery of Basil Hopkins French's death.

And the mystery of Miss L'Hommedieu.

An hour later, returning to the kitchen with his pocket crammed full of lists, he told Gussie, "There were no poetry books. Actually I'd thought of finding one all lace and chiffon for her."

Gussie gave him an enigmatic glance. "Lace and chiffon? She was an actress for a short time, you know, out of work, homeless, and living on the streets when Miss Thale found her."

He was not surprised; he realized that nothing about Miss L'Hommedieu—or anyone—could ever surprise him now.

"And had she been a good actress?" he asked.

"A good actress?" Gussie smiled. "On the stage, no."

"Ah," said Andrew, nodding, and he went out into the garden to find Tarragon and tell her that his last nightmare had ended, that Miss L'Hommedieu had left behind her a gift of enormous value for him, a puzzle to solve, a mystery to unravel, a story that excited him, a book to write. *Had* to write. *Must* write.

Nor would Miss L'Hommedieu be at all surprised, he thought, that by chance it was he who had opened her trunk. She would only say, borrowing freely again from Anatole France, that Chance was the word God used when he wished to remain anonymous.